THE AFRIKANER

A NOVEL

ESSENTIAL PROSE SERIES 161

Canada Council for the Arts | Conseil des Arts du Canada

ONTARIO ARTS COUNCIL
CONSEIL DES ARTS DE L'ONTARIO

an Ontario government agency
un organisme du gouvernement de l'Ontario

Canada

Guernica Editions Inc. acknowledges the support of the Canada Council for the Arts and the Ontario Arts Council. The Ontario Arts Council is an agency of the Government of Ontario.

We acknowledge the financial support of the Government of Canada.

Arianna Dagnino

THE AFRIKANER

A NOVEL

GUERNICA EDITIONS
TORONTO • BUFFALO • LANCASTER (U.K.)
2019

Michael Mirolla, editor
David Moratto, cover and interior design
Cover image: Painting titled *Ultimo orizzonte* by Romano Dagnino
Cover photo: Stefano Gulmanelli.

Guernica Editions Inc.
1569 Heritage Way, Oakville, (ON), Canada L6M 2Z7
2250 Military Road, Tonawanda, N.Y. 14150-6000 U.S.A.
www.guernicaeditions.com

Distributors:
University of Toronto Press Distribution,
5201 Dufferin Street, Toronto (ON), Canada M3H 5T8
Gazelle Book Services, White Cross Mills
High Town, Lancaster LA1 4XS U.K.

First edition.
Printed in Canada.

Legal Deposit — First Quarter
Library of Congress Catalog Card Number: 2018956337
Library and Archives Canada Cataloguing in Publication
Dagnino, Arianna, 1963-, author
The Afrikaner / Arianna Dagnino.

(Essential prose series ; 161)
Issued in print and electronic formats.
ISBN 978-1-77183-357-8 (softcover).--ISBN 978-1-77183-358-5 (EPUB).--
ISBN 978-1-77183-359-2 (Kindle)

I. Title. II. Series: Essential prose series ; 161

PS8607.A279A74 2019 C813'.6 C2018-905027-6 C2018-905028-4

To "the rains down in Africa"
and to my children, Morgana and Leonardo

On ne voit bien qu'avec le cœur;
L'essentiel est invisible pour les yeux.
It is only with the heart that one can see rightly;
What is essential is invisible to the eye.
—Antoine de Saint-Exupéry

It is often in the most hidden of places
that we find the richest and most interesting stories.
—Anonymous

If I had done this, if I had said that,
in the end you are always more tormented
by what you didn't do than what you did,
actions already performed can always be rationalized in time,
the neglected deed might have changed the world.
—Damon Galgut

CONTENTS

GLOSSARY

Afrikaans (Afrikaans): The language descended from Dutch spoken by the Afrikaner in South Africa and Namibia. Earlier on, it was also known as "kitchen Dutch." The emergence of Afrikaans as a language in the former Dutch colony of Cape Town in South Africa started as early as 1685. In 1925, it was recognized as an official language and was closely tied to apartheid. Afrikaans, like all other 10 national languages of South Africa, is now protected by the Constitution. About 7.2 million people speak Afrikaans as a native language, and a further 8-15 million speak it as a second language.

Afrikaner (Afrikaans): A descendant of early settlers from northern Europe (mainly Calvinists from the Netherlands and, in much smaller percentages, religious refugees from France and Germany) who established themselves in the Western Cape area between 1652 and 1795, when the region was under the influence of the Dutch East India Company. See also, *Boer.*

Ag! (Afrikaans): 'Ah!,' 'Oh!,' 'Oh no!'

Aia (Afrikaans): Nanny, ayah.

Amagqira (Xhosa): Female shamanic healer.

Asseblief (Afrikaans): 'Please.'

Baas (Afrikaans): Master, boss. Often used by Black or Coloured people when addressing Whites in positions of authority under apartheid.

Bakkie (South African English, slang): A pick-up truck, a 4×4 with no rear hood.

Baster (Afrikaans): An ethnic minority of Namibia; its members are the mixed-race descendants of early Dutch settlers and Khoikhoi women.

Biltong (Afrikaans): Dried, salted and cured meat in strips.

Bittereinders (Afrikaans): 'The irreconcilables.' Supporters of the Boer cause who wished to continue the fight during the commando phase of the Second Boer War (1899-1902) even though they knew their end was near.

Bobotie (Afrikaans): Traditional Cape-Malay dish; a mix of curried ground meat, spice and fruit.

Boer (Afrikaans): A 'farmer' of Dutch, German or Huguenot descent. Today, descendants of the Boers are commonly referred to as Afrikaners.

Boerewors (Afrikaans): A popular, traditional sausage; usually a coarsely-ground mixture of beef and pork seasoned with various spices.

Braai (Afrikaans): Barbecue.

Coloured (English): Coloureds are people of mixed lineage with origins from Europe, Asia (in particular Malay slaves from Dutch colonies in the East Indies), and various Khoisan and Bantu tribes of Southern Africa.

Dagga (Afrikaans): Slang name for cannabis, marijuana, weed.

Dankie (Afrikaans): 'Thank you.'

Dorp (Afrikaans): Village.

Duiker (Afrikaans): Small antelope native to Sub-Saharan Africa. Scientific name: *Sylvicapra grimmia.*

eGoli (Sotho): 'The place of gold'; the local name by which Johannesburg was known during the gold rush that led to the establishment of the city in 1886.

Fokkin (Afrikaans): 'Fucking.'

Gemmerkoekies (Afrikaans): Ginger cookies.

Gemsbok (Afrikaans): Oryx. Scientific name: *Oryx gazella*. A kind of antelope with long sable horns.

Goed (Afrikaans): 'Well,' 'Good.'

Goeiemôre (Afrikaans): 'Good morning.'

Goeienaand (Afrikaans): 'Good evening.'

Goeienag (Afrikaans): 'Good night.'

Hadedah (South African English): A grayish brown African ibis.

Hensoppers (Afrikaans): 'Quitters'; lit., 'hands uppers.' Derogatory term by which Afrikaners would refer to those among them who, during the Second Anglo-Boer War (1899-1902), surrendered or defected to the English usually doing so by raising their hands.

Highveld (English, from Afrikaans *hooge veld*): The inland plateau of southern Africa, lying mostly between 1200m and 1800m above sea-level.

Ja (Afrikaans): 'Yes.'

Ju/'Hoansi: A Bushmen tribe belonging to the !Kung group; its members inhabit the Nyae Nyae region (previously also known as Bushmanland), in north-eastern Namibia.

Kaffir (Afrikaans): 'Nigger' (derogative). The term comes from the Arabic *kafir*, unbeliever.

Karos (Khoikhoi and Afrikaans): Animal skin used as a saddlebag, blanket or garment.

Khoisan (English): The name *Khoisan* is a blend of Khoikhoi and San, two groups who share similar cultures and languages. The Khoikhoi (also known as Hottentots), pastoralists, and the San (or Bushmen), hunter-gatherers, were the first inhabitants of the region south of the Zambezi River.

Klim uit! (Afrikaans): 'Get out!'

Kokerboom (Afrikaans): Quiver tree. A succulent plant indigenous to southern Africa. Scientific name: *Aloe dichotoma.* It's called *kokerboom* because the Khoisan would use their trunks to make quivers to hold their arrows.

Kom (Afrikaans): 'Come.'

Koppie (Afrikaans): A small hill in a generally flat area.

Kraal (Afrikaans): A traditional African village. Also, an enclosure for cattle or other livestock.

!Kung: Bushmen of Northern Namibia who share the same language and customs. They are part of the San people who live mostly on the Western edge of the Kalahari Desert. The exclamation point in the *!Kung*'s name indicates that the "k" is pronounced with a click sound. Click sounds are distinctive of Khoisan languages.

Laager (Afrikaans): Encampment. Traditionally, a camp or encampment formed by a circle of wagons lashed or chained together for defensive purposes; particularly an encampment of emigrant Boers (see, *Trekboers*).

Loop (Afrikaans): 'Go!' 'Walk!' 'Go ahead!'

Mies (Afrikaans): Miss; a white woman, especially an employer.

Mejuffrou (Afrikaans): Miss.

Nagmaal (Afrikaans): Communion. In the Dutch Reformed churches, the sacrament of Holy Communion; the communion service; the occasion, usually four times a year, during which this service is held.

Nee (Afrikaans): 'No.'

N/om: According to Bushmen's lore, the energy source that gives life to the universe and to all its creatures.

Noré (!Kung): The area traditionally inhabited by a Bushmen clan.

Nou goed (Afrikaans): 'It's ok,' 'Well well.'

Olifante (Afrikaans): Elephants.

Oom (Afrikaans): Uncle. Used as a respectful or affectionate form of address for an elderly man, not necessarily referring to a blood relation.

Ouma (Afrikaans): Grandma, old mum. Denoting a parent's mother, or, informally, any other elderly woman.

Ousus (Afrikaans): 'Older sister.' A term of affection.

Ovambo (Pshiwambo): Ethnic group belonging to the Bantu peoples. The Ovambos are the largest ethnic group of Namibia.

Padkos (Afrikaans): Food for the journey, provisions.

Panga (Zulu and Kiswahili): Machete.

Plaas (Afrikaans): Farm.

Potjiekos (Afrikaans): A traditional Boer dish; a stew cooked in a three-legged cast-iron pot over an open fire.

Predikant (Afrikaans): A minister of a Dutch Reformed church.

Qat: Native plant to the Horn of Africa and the Arabian Peninsula whose leaves are traditionally chewed as a social custom. Its stimulant effects are analogous to the coca leaves in South America.

Rooibos (Afrikaans): 'Red bush'; a broom-like member of the *Fabaceae* family of plants growing in South Africa's fynbos. Its leaves are used to make a caffeine free herbal tea.

Rooi gevaar (Afrikaans): 'The red peril.' Communism. The perceived threat of international communism to the

Afrikaner community of South Africa. The political tactic of encouraging an unreasonable fear of communism.

San: See, *Khoisan*.

Sangoma (Zulu): Shaman. Name given to Xhosa and Zulu traditional diviners.

Shangaan (English): A member of people of Zulu and Tsonga origin.

Shebeen (from the Irish *síbín*): Unlicensed drinking establishment usually located in townships during apartheid.

Sjambok (Afrikaans): A long, stiff whip, formally cut from rhinoceros or hippo hide.

Sotho: One of the eleven official ethnic groups of South Africa.

Stoep (Afrikaans): Traditional terrace or veranda in Cape Dutch-style farmsteads.

Swart gevaar (Afrikaans): 'Black danger.' A perceived threat posed by black people to whites.

Totsiens (Afrikaans): 'Till we meet again,' 'See you.' An informal expression used on parting.

Trekboere (Afrikaans): Wandering farmers.

Tsamma (Nama): A bitter wild melon, of the species *Citrullus lanatus*, native to the Kalahari Desert.

Tsonga (English): Bantu ethnic group of southern Africa.

Tsotsitaal (South African English, slang): A mixed language mainly spoken in the townships of Gauteng province, such as Soweto. From *Tsotsi* (in the Nguni languages it means 'criminal' but also 'street smart') and *Taal* ('language' in Afrikaans).

Tswana: Ethnic group belonging to the Bantu people.

Uitlander (Afrikaans): Foreigner.

Veld (Afrikaans): Open grassland or scrubland interspersed with trees.

Volk (Afrikaans): People, members of a particular group.

Waarom? (Afrikaans): 'Why?'

Welkom (Afrikaans): 'Welcome.'

Xhosa: A major sub-division of the Nguni group, comprising those peoples traditionally living in what is now the Eastern Cape Province.

Yebo (Zulu): 'Yes.'

Zol (South African English, slang): A hand-rolled marijuana cigarette.

Zulu (English): Bantu ethnic group of southern Africa and the largest ethnic group of South Africa.

PROLOGUE

"Klim uit!"

The guy in the hood shouts the order in Afrikaans. Then he sees my blank stare and repeats it in English.

"Get out of the caaar!! Move!!"

The sparse street lamps shed a disquieting light, islands of incandescence exposing the city's nakedness. On this night, just like many others, the city centre is deserted. There's not a soul to be seen except for the three shadows now descending on me out of a world of darkness. I should have known it was coming: One can't gamble with destiny for too long. Besides, "this is Jo'burg," as everyone here is keen to remind me, "one of the most dangerous cities in the world."

My fault: absent-minded as usual, driving at night and stopping at the red light. They warned me about that too. Acquaintances, workmates, even people I had just met at the bar or a party would repeat it time and again, like a mantra to ward off bad luck—more for themselves than out of real concern for me. "In downtown, at night, red lights mean nothing. Slow down, but don't ever stop. And always keep your eye on the rear-view mirror to see who's coming."

What a way to go out! Four lines on page two of the *Star* among the daily victims of hijackings: "Dario Oldani, a young Italian researcher in South Africa for the past two years, was killed on the corner of Commissioner and Rissik Streets in the Central Business District. His car, a white Golf GTX, was stolen."

Somehow, I find myself out of the car with my arms thrust out in front of me on the hood. Someone is frisking me, rapidly and professionally.

"I'm a foreigner," I try explaining. "I'm not South African."

"Does it make you a better White?" the guy removing the wallet from my trouser pocket says.

"Asshole!" another voice, muffled by a balaclava, shouts.

With my head firmly pushed downwards, all I can see are the bottom halves of my aggressors' coats and the Reeboks on their feet. Things are happening fast. Yet, I see them unfold as if in slow motion, each detail bursting full-blown in my head.

Suddenly, in the midst of the commotion, police sirens pierce the night.

"Go! Go!" shouts one of the three hooded figures, already behind the wheel.

The one who was frisking me jerks me back from the car. I stagger, then stumble on the pavement and fall to the ground with my face in the garbage, among the remains of a day spent on the street by ordinary people. All those faceless men and women peeling bananas, wrapping peanuts in old newspaper, smoking cheap cigarettes, peeing against the wall, sleeping on stone steps. I hear the screech of tires from somewhere not far off. The cavalry is closing in. Now I'll wake up and think of this as just a bad dream. I will no longer have my car, but who cares: I'll be alive, surveying the vast, intensely blue sky of another day on the Highveld.

By now the three men are in the car. I'm pulling himself up, with an effort. In the fall, I must have twisted my ankle. I lean against the wall, half-bent in pain. I raise my eyes and, instinctively, turn towards the car already speeding away. The dim light of the street lamp reveals an arm coming out of the back window. The hand holds a gun, pointed at me. It fires.

—1—

AN ENCOUNTER IN THE KAROO

NOTHINGNESS. SHE HAS been driving for hours on end across this nothingness. When she pulls to the side of the road and turns off the engine, the sun has already begun its red descent into the horizon. She steps out into the dry heat. The stony expanse of the Karoo stretches out for kilometres on end—illusory and timeless, like a de Chirico landscape. The stillness is broken only by the hushed breathing of the radiator. She walks away from the vehicle, oblivious to the scratches on her legs as she makes her way through the thorny bushes and the sharp yellow grass. She goes deep into her imaginary canvas, then stops. The sound of her footsteps fades out. There remains only silence. Deep, primordial silence. That's all she is aching for.

❁❁❁

"*Goeiemôre,* Zoe."

She flinches. She has been sitting on her solitary rock for quite a while now, watching the sky veer into blood orange, and hasn't heard any footsteps. The initial fright turns quickly into disbelief: *that* voice! Could it really be *him*?

She turns and there, a few steps from her, stands the

shortest of men—no taller than a metre and a half. His dark olive skin is wrinkled and shrivelled like a walnut shell. Under the visor of a battered baseball cap, she makes out the slants of his eyes and, out of the shade, his slightly restrained, dignified smile.

She jumps up to greet him.

"Koma! *Ek sien jou*!"

The old Bushman comes up to her with light steps and clasps her hands in his.

"I see you too, *Mejuffrou*."

Startled by the dream-like apparition, she briefly looks past Koma, trying to figure out where he may have come from. All she can see is a boundless stretch of bare country.

"*Oom*, what are you doing *here*?"

"I visited friends living on a farm over there," he says pointing to the east with his arm stretched out, the back of his hand facing up.

Her memory brings her back to 1986.

She is a graduate student spending the summer in Schmidtsdrift. The Army has chosen the nearby military base to relocate the Bushmen soldiers who fought in the frontier wars in Namibia. They have been brought here with their families, away from the public eye. There are about 4,000 of them, making it the largest San community left in Africa, and Zoe got permission to study their customs and way of life. On the very first day of her stay, the Base Captain introduces her to Koma, the !Kung shaman, one of the best trackers in the South African Army.

"Still at the camp, Koma?"

"*Ja*, too old to work on a *plaas*."

How old is he? Fifty, sixty? Even he couldn't tell.

"You might be too old to work on a farm, *Oom*, but you don't seem too old to go on foot across the Karoo. When did you leave?"

"Three days ago. It will take me another four days to be back," he says as if it were the most natural thing in the world.

"I can give you a ride."

"*Nee*. Walking is good. It has taken me back to the lost days, when I was a young hunter."

As he talks, Koma lets his eyes roam across the landscape.

For a while, they share the stillness of the place, drawn by the same sense of wonder, the same urge of wandering. Eventually, with his gaze still fixed into the horizon, the old shaman says: "Your heart is aching."

She is taken aback. Startled by the oddness of their encounter, Zoe has momentarily forgotten the cause of her flight. She keeps quiet, looking down at the dust on her boots, forced back into reality. She is trying to answer but something is lodged in her throat.

"The arrows of sorrow hit me hard this time," she manages to say at last.

Another long spell of silence. Zoe glances at the old man but can make out only his profile in the naked light of the veld.

"At times, we need to be like the weed, which bends in the wind," Koma eventually says.

She sits back on her rock. There is no point in asking him to elaborate: The old shaman would look away, pretending not to have heard her. Besides, she doesn't want to plead for clarity.

She would rather hush her mind a little longer.

Instinctively, she finds herself following the old man's gaze, as the sun heads toward its daily death.

After a long while she stands up and walks to the car. She pulls from her backpack three packages of *biltong* she bought for the trip and takes the bottle of water lying on the passenger seat; then goes back to Koma and hands him the dried meat and the water.

"They will come in handy."

"*Goed.*"

The old man slips the offerings in his knapsack.

"*Oom*, how come our paths have crossed here, in the middle of a desert?"

"The magic is in every moment of life, *Mejuffrou*. I thought you took note of this in the little book you used to carry everywhere."

Koma clasps her hands, then goes on his way without turning around.

She watches him walk away, a small dark figure against a scarlet backdrop, the pace slow and measured. He is still wearing his old uniform, all patched and worn-out, and a pair of sandals made from truck tires.

"*Totsiens, Oom,*" she finally says, still feeling the bushman's dry and nervous strength around her wrists.

She moves towards the car. The light is fast draining from the sky. If she sits tight, she will be in Bloemfontein before dark settles in.

❁❁❁

"Take a few days off, Zoe. Indeed, as many as you need." Born out of genuine concern, Johan Kuyper's tone of voice hadn't left much space for objection. Her boss, the Director of the Bernard Price Institute for Palaeontological Research at the University of Witwatersrand, was right nonetheless: She would do better to go back home for a while, down to the Cape.

So here she is, on the road home.

The university will take care of everything, Kuyper assured her, including the red tape to repatriate Dario's body. As much as she tries, she can't stop seeing her lover's parents at the airport being handed their son inside a coffin. But then, everything she does, touches or thinks inevitably brings her back to him, to what his death means.

Just a few hours before the car rental agent delivered in front of her house in Johannesburg a white Golf GTX. She gasped: the same kind of car Dario had. It would mean driving for 1,400 kilometres with her lover's ghost still in the driver's seat. Her immediate reaction had been to call the car rental and ask for a different car. On second thought, though, she decided otherwise. Painful as it might be, she would rather drive picturing Dario's hands laid on hers, holding gently to the steering wheel.

She has left the city in an anguished rush. Johannesburg, to her, will never be the same again. It has given her so much, but has also taken away everything in one fell swoop. She has driven the first hundred kilometres in a state of semi-consciousness, as the landscape started undressing with phlegmatic composure. The further she went into it, the fewer houses, fewer hills, fewer trees, fewer people, fewer cars she encountered. And she hoped she could do the same, slowly stripping down to clean, desert air. On other occasions, when facing a crisis, she had been able to do "the trick," as her brother calls it. She would leave behind everything—sorrows, worries, meanness. Till, in the end, what had seemed a raw pain, an unbearable angst, would dissolve in the dryness of the veld. The Karoo would drain her to the point of nothingness, until the suffering would disperse in the wind, along with her aching soul.

But this time it's different. What she thought were the figments of some female ancestor have proven to be real. Deadly real. The blights of a daunting past have caught up with her too.

On impulse, terrified by her thoughts, she turns on the radio. What a mistake! The notes of a sad love song fill the car. All those memories, those moments of sweetness never to return. She slams the radio off. Too late. Grief seizes her. She begins to yell at the windshield, trying in vain to expel the beast. She presses on the gas pedal and rushes into the twilight. She keeps pushing, wildly, as her vision blurs and the road ahead becomes an ever-narrower strip of asphalt. All it would take is a slight swerve of the wheel. Then, it would all be over: the pain, the shame. Instead, she slows down, back to safety. And she hates herself: She has not the courage, not even now. She's just a coward, a petty human being pitying herself instead of crying for her dead lover. It hurts, but she can't deny the selfishness of her tears, of the question vexing her: Why go on living now? Dario has taught her to speak the language of seduction, look straight into the eyes of desire, fall in love. All this is gone. Forever lost. It will be a wasted life.

A wasted body.

— 2 —
DEATH

Zoe is lying in bed in her hotel room in Bloemfontein. Alone. In the dusk. Her eyes wide open, her mind racing back to events that happened less than 48 hours ago. But they might date back a week, a month, a year. She thrashes about in a blur of memories, moves, broken images where time seems to have collapsed onto itself.

It's early in the morning when Piet knocks on her lab's door. He doesn't wait for her answer to enter, closing the door soundlessly behind him. At this time of the day, the room is bathed in light as the rays of a late spring sunshine filter in, caressing walls and objects with golden dust. She looks up and nods at her long-time friend and colleague, then examines for the umpteenth time what remains of the hominid skull in front of her as she is about to put in place a last fragment in its reconstructed cheekbone.

An hour earlier, washing hastily in the restroom, she had pretended not to see her messy hair, the shadows under her eyes, the bare landscape of her cheeks and lips. Yet, she has never felt better. Besides, it's a pivotal moment in her career: She is about to give shape again to Lady J, awakening her from her Palaeolithic sleep. Each element of their ancestor's ossified identity contains a passage in human evolution and now her secrets, still hidden in the jaws and teeth worn down by use and time, will be gradually revealed in learned hypotheses. Were she able to speak, Lady J would tell them how, why and when humans rejected the kingdom of the apes to take on a long, uncharted journey, leading to the tragic awareness of infamy and death, but also to the uplifting sense of beauty and moral bravery.

Glancing across at Piet again, Zoe notices a certain awkwardness in his manner. Nothing like his usual easy camaraderie. He stands still at the end of the table, as if in deep contemplation of what lies on it: a dozen hominid skulls, volumes on anatomy, microscopes, empty coffee cups, a bra, the remains of two takeaway pizzas.

"What's up, Piet?" she asks.

At that, his large head with its permanently dishevelled fair hair jerks up, and the young man starts blurting out words in a confused manner:

"You were keeping it secret, Zoe … but just about everyone in the Department knew … well … you were seeing each other … Dario … he confided in me … just a few days ago … he was smitten with you …"

Still crouched over her fossil, she abruptly stops all that rambling with a simple question:

"Was?"

There is a long silence. Too long. She slowly looks up at him.

Piet's answer reaches her as if piercing the air through dense mist, past a thick forest—his voice low and hoarse, his chin almost touching his chest. "They killed him, Zoe. Last night, downtown. A hijacking."

She feels her lips close tightly, her limbs suddenly numb, as if the blood had instantly drained from them. Her eyes shift back down to the workbench. With incongruous calmness and a steady hand, she puts in place the final piece into Lady J's skull. What an odd reaction for a woman who has just been told her man is dead: The thought flashes through her mind and stuns her with its brutality. Then, all at once, she feels dizzy, weak. She bends over leaning on the table for support. Piet hurries towards her, although with the circumspection he would use with a wounded animal. Moving from behind he helps her to stand and find comfort in his embrace. Despite her distress, she cannot help noticing the swift gesture with which her friend frees his right hand and pushes Lady J's skull out of her way.

Piet has insisted on giving her a lift home. She remains silent throughout the journey, blankly staring out of the car window. They drive through sleepy streets lined with umbrella-shaped jacarandas, the purple of their blooming already fading. As they turn into 7th Street in Melville, the bukinist, *an old Ukrainian, recognizes Zoe and waves in greeting through his half-open door. She doesn't respond.*

A few minutes later Piet brings the car to a stop in front of her house. He squints slightly, as short-sighted people do when they resist wearing glasses, then quickly walks around the car to open the door for her.

"You know I'm not going to ask you in," she says softly but firmly as she gets out.

"You shouldn't be left by yourself, not today."

She doesn't reply. She briefly kisses his unshaven cheek and turns to open the gate, moving out of his line of vision.

For a while she wanders around the house without purpose, seeing everything as if from an infinite distance;

then she throws herself under the shower, gulps down two Rohypnol tablets and curls up on the couch.

She is awakened a few hours later by the insistent ringing of the doorbell. When she opens the door, somewhat dazed, she is still in her bathrobe. Standing before her in the late afternoon light is a man in civilian clothes, the butt of a pistol sticking out from under his jacket.

"Mejuffrow *Zoe du Plessis? Detective Inspector Ian Klopper," he quickly says in Afrikaans, showing his badge.*

"Yes, it's me," she answers in English. Afrikaans is the language of domestic intimacy and she doesn't feel like speaking it with this man. English will place an invisible barrier between them.

"May I come in?"

The police officer has switched to English quite easily, quickly reading her silent intention. Like everyone else, he too has had to adjust to the times. In the new South Africa the language of the oppressor is no longer in fashion. She herself uses it only with her closest relations.

The DI is a stout man with a reddish face, thick blond moustache and beer-drinker's paunch. When he starts asking questions about her relationship with Dario, she averts her eyes.

"How long had you been dating?"

"About six months," she says.

Klopper has made no effort to avoid the accusatory tone in his voice. Nonetheless she can picture him exchanging comments with colleagues and friends at his next Sunday braai, *as he busies himself turning steaks with the barbecue fork, drinking Castle from the can: "Serves her right, screwing a* fokking uitlander, *an Italian looking for his fifteen-minute South African thrill. What the guy was doing in the Central Business District at three in the morning anyway is beyond me. Did he want to see what has become of the city centre now that the* kaffirs *are in charge?* Goed, *now he knows. All these erudite liberal Europeans who come to teach us how to live in the new South Africa and are dying for a dinner in a* shebeen *in Soweto. Intercultural experiences, they call them. That's one less to worry about."*

"They told me at the Department that you stayed there working all night. When did Dr. Oldani leave?"

"Around two o'clock, I believe. Two thirty perhaps," she answers glancing at the stiff collar of his shirt cutting into his stubby neck. The too tight tie doesn't help either.

"What on earth was he doing in the CBD after dark?"

Here we go, Zoe tells herself, knowing where this conversation will lead.

"He was going home," she replies. She presumes that by now the DI knows Dario lived in Rosettenville, to the south of the city centre, 'among the Whites who didn't make it,' as he would often remark. "Driving through the CBD is the fastest route, as you well know."

"Answer me this, then: Did your colleague know the risk he was running by entering the city centre at that time of night?"

He did, of course. Even the most liberal-minded colleagues at the Department seemed eager to remind him that with the changed political climate even this city "has gone African."

She pauses and, once again, sees the dark, empty streets, the tramps wandering about in the shadows, the red glow of the fires people would light in petrol drums to keep warm.

"He liked gambling with his life, our professor," Klopper

says as he puts a finger inside his shirt collar and undoes the top button with an impatient gesture.

These words, or perhaps the contemptuous tone in his voice, make her snap.

"That's preposterous, Inspector. Dr. Oldani wasn't some sort of irresponsible fool. He was a scholar and this city fascinated him. He wanted to understand its historical wounds, its complexity."

Klopper doesn't bother to repress a sneer.

She suddenly falls quiet. How stupid of me. What is the purpose of such a pedantic tirade? Why bother trying to explain to this man Dario's social theories on the dynamics of power, conflict, dispossession?

The Detective Inspector watches her in silence, visibly disappointed. He knows she will never give him this satisfaction: She will never acknowledge the evidence of an attitude she too considers rash, excessively casual, presumptuously European. Yes, she feels betrayed by her lover—for not having understood Africa, for not realizing where he was, for having ruined her life as well as his own. She resents Dario's behaviour since, with his negligence, he allowed fate to materialize. But she won't admit it. Not to the man in front of her.

Thus, she finally lowers her gaze and leaves to the police officer the pleasure of uttering the ritual words: "This is Africa, Miss."

True, this is Africa, and the worse things get, the more Klopper and his ilk may indulge their subequatorial cynicism.

Klopper has taken his leave and Zoe is alone now, in the dusk. She goes back to the bathroom, her senses fully alert.

She grabs the scissors and, strand after strand, lets her long red hair fall to the ground. In the silence, only the zack! zack! zack! of the blades accompanies the workings of her mind, as grief makes its way in. For the first time in her life, she allowed a man to love her without holding anything back. But this came at a price.

Dario's death wasn't a mere accident. Now she knows.

The sequence of the last dreadful events keeps playing in her head. Over and over. An ongoing flashback running on a morbid loop, which Zoe seems unable to stop. Unless sleep comes to her aid.

— 3 —
CANDLES IN THE NIGHT

"André? It's me, Zoe."

"*Ousus, howzit?*"

The warmth of his voice has the sudden effect of a balm. Although she is the eldest, Zoe looks up to her brother. At thirty, and after having elegantly survived their troubled childhood, he runs the wine estate they inherited from their parents. His bemused and contagious enthusiasm has kept him afloat. No matter how hard life may hit him, he bounces back. She has never heard him bemoan his problems or rail—for that matter—against the country's state of affairs—neither before, at the height of apartheid, nor now that Blacks are openly seeking retaliation and redressing the wrongs done to them by Whites. He seems to belong to an unending line of African fatalists—those feeling that "the hand of history" dictates the game, in spite of how each chooses to play it.

"I'm coming to the Finistère."

"About time!" Then, after a slight pause: "You sound strange, though ... Something wrong?"

She bites her lip, her eyes suddenly misty.

"Come on, *ousus,* spit it out."

"Not now, not over the phone."

"I'll fetch you at the airport, then. Did you book your flight?"

"I'm driving. I'm in Bloemfontein right now."

"Why would you want to schlep all the way over here?"

She keeps quiet.

"Let me guess. The healing power of deserts—that little obsession of yours."

There is another pause, in which she thinks she can hear André's distant breathing.

"Zoe ... what happened?"

She bites her lip harder, till it hurts, but she hangs on: "Wait for me, will you?"

There is silence on the other end. She senses André is trying to assess the situation: Should I try to reach her in the Karoo? Or prompt her to confide in me? Only to reach the same conclusion she would come to if she were in his place: Let her be.

"Are you sure you can make it with that old Beetle of yours?"

She smiles sadly as she stares out of her hotel room window at the white Golf GTX parked outside.

"I've rented a car."

Silence again.

"Will you stop at the Drostdy?"

"I guess so."

"*Goed.* Take care, *ousus.*"

❁❁❁

After having thrust her clothes bag into the car's trunk, Zoe makes the automatic gesture of tying her hair in a knot on the back of her head as she has done hundreds of times, but stops with her arms in mid-air, suddenly realizing there is no longer anything to tie.

It's late in the morning when she drives out of town. The sky is an irritating blue, the sunlight downright outrageous, rendering the squatter camps besieging the outskirts almost acceptable. A golden halo enwraps waste piles, open sewers, rags, stray dogs, dark-skinned children playing barefoot in the dust. She rushes past rows of tin shacks reflecting the rays of another realm. Then the Karoo opens again in front of her with its monotony of scrub and sun-baked plains. For over a thousand kilometres only solitary *koppies* break the horizon with their dumb, flat-topped shapes, until the grasslands give way to the vertical asperity of the Swartberg Mountains, down down south.

It takes another five-hour drive for Zoe to reach the small *dorp* of Graaff-Reinet. In the late eighteenth century, this out-of-time town was the first outpost in the interior of those settlers who left the Cape region seeking freedom and adventure, away from the restrictions of the Dutch East India Company. Since then, "the pearl of the Karoo" hasn't changed much. The desert space keeps protecting its rough frontier spirit and the Cape Dutch style of its buildings. "One has just to remove the rare cars and replace them with ox carts to be brought back to that era," Zoe remembers writing in her field journal when, early in her career, she spent two months in Graaff-Reinet, using it as the basis for a series of fossil excavations that would prove fruitless.

Though disappointing in terms of scientific results, she now considers that time as one of the most serene in her life. Her desert baptism took place among the hot rocks rising just over the settlement. It's there that, for the first time, she encountered the power of geographical emptiness, the non-place where, as the Bushmen say, you can hear the stars sing. She still remembers how, through Bushmen's eyes, she then looked at the madness of it all, the way people crammed themselves in megalopolises while their souls still needed the religiousness of absolutes.

Zoe has parked outside the Drostdy. Before taking in travellers by post and modern-day tourists, the former residence of the local magistrate witnessed the coming and going of reconnaissance parties, destitute farmers, migrant sheep-shearers, slaves in chains, greedy colonials: all souls adrift, straddling the midriff of the country along long-lost tracks. She stops to gaze at the inn's white-washed façade, central gable and dark-grey thatch of dried wild reeds.

Once inside, as she checks in, the owners recognize Zoe from previous stays and invite her to have drinks in their private quarters. She politely declines the offer. She isn't done for the day yet and has to rush, as in less than an hour it will all be over. Racing out of Graaff-Reinet Zoe takes the dirt road to the Karoo Natural Reserve. The access gate is still open, as she'd hoped. She leaves the car at the bottom of the escarpment and takes the steep path leading to the central peak. It takes her no more than fifteen minutes to reach the bluff only to realize, with disappointment, that the best vantage point is taken. A man up there, in dark cotton pants and white shirt, is looking down into the valley that once stood, with its moon-like scapes, in the centre of Gondwana before the continents started drifting apart. Whether he heard her coming, she cannot tell. Zoe crouches quietly on a boulder slightly set back, in a spot nearly as dominant as his.

All around them, bizarre formations of dolerite rise from the grasslands: petrified organ pipes brushed by strokes of sunset light. The curved line of the horizon hangs from the sky like a giant seashell. In the silence, only the wailing cry of golden eagles can be heard, as the birds of prey soar in the wake of invisible updrafts. She sits there, motionless, watching a scene almost unchanged for millions of years. Slowly, her mind glides away and she relives that moment. Their last moment.

On the dot of midnight, Dario turns off the laboratory lights, leaving only the feeble glow of the microscope, and says: "This is your time, Dr. Du Plessis." Bent over her fossils, Zoe doesn't see that a few minutes earlier her lover had been clearing a space among the skulls on the bench. Filled with desire, he now pulls her to him and lifts her onto that blue Formica island surrounded by a sea of bones. Slowly and deliberately, he undoes the buttons of her lab coat. With a sudden flush, Zoe feels again his hands cupped around her breasts, his tongue warm and moist between her thighs. She remembers the feeling of floating suspended on the thread of their pleasure, her back arched above the blue island like a bridge to infinity.

Turning her head to the side, she is confronted by one of

those ugly hominid skulls, but it doesn't bother her—actually, it even increases her arousal.

That's what we were, Dario: Two modern specimens of *Homo sapiens* re-enacting a ritual lost in the night of time. And that's what we did: We performed a dance macabre balancing the life in our loins with the death of those enigmatic bones.

The sun finally sinks with its crimson farewell. Now, the darkness will quickly enwrap the scene.

The stranger doesn't move, not even now.

Zoe quietly walks away, drowning in the navy blue of the coming night.

❁❁❁

One hour and a shower later, she walks into the dining hall of the Drostdy Hotel. Nothing seems to have changed in this room of thick shadows with no artificial lighting. Despite the daily care of silent black hands, the patina of time has left its mark on this place deliberately left behind. The wooden floors creak with every step, wrought-iron chandeliers glow in the light of candles. A young black maid, dressed up in immaculate lace apron and bonnet, greets Zoe with a hint of a bow.

The room is half empty. An elderly couple have finished their meal and are about to leave. A solitary guest occupies a corner table. Zoe recognizes the stranger of the sunset by his clothing and the line of his shoulders. She is not surprised to find him here, the only place to have a proper meal in town. The man is rapidly taking notes on a black-leathered pad. He stops, stares for a little while into the void through a pair of gold-rimmed lenses and then goes back to his writing, trying to catch on the fly what he saw in his mind's eye.

Crossing the room, Zoe walks past the carved wooden furniture, the pendulum that tolls like Big Ben in London, the gray stone fireplace. She throws a last glance at the three-arm candelabra on the tables before heading for the outdoor patio, where she asked to have her meal served. Normally, she would have books with her—"Another way to cut the world off when you find yourself out there, in the world," as André says. But this is no ordinary journey. She's not here to make the most of her time; she's here to annihilate it.

The waitress is back a few minutes later with a basket of fresh bread and a glass of Sauvignon Blanc from the Finistère Wine Estate.

"From the owners," she says.

Before tasting the wine, Zoe inhales its scent. Less refined than that of a European one, she knows, but in that fruity bouquet, which mixes cedar with papaya, green melon with fresh honey, she finds her childhood again, the colours of the Cape in autumn, the melancholy of a rough ocean. They say people drink to forget; when she does it, which doesn't happen often, it's to remember. They also say that children are not aware of their happiness. Perhaps. But, as a child, Zoe savoured that feeling of untroubled blitheness aware that it would soon be lost. She would watch adults closely, see their gazes weighed down with nostalgia, hardened by life, and understand that there wouldn't be second chances. Looking back at it now, that spark of childhood wisdom had something disturbingly premature, as if it contained within it the seeds of an omen, or of an inevitable retaliation: *You cannot be happy for too long, or too often, in your life.*

She hears the gravel crunch a few feet away and sees the stranger coming out into the night. She senses his presence, but she is not annoyed by this. In fact, it's as if she were still alone in the semi-darkness, or with a person whom she has known all along. The shells of their silences are touching without friction, like those of two old friends intent on fishing in the early hours. She hears the click of a lighter and, a few moments later, the aroma of Gitanes tobacco — the same brand her brother smokes — fills the air. The stranger casually tidies up his tuft of blondish hair. Then he looks around and sees her.

"*Goeienaand*," he says, letting out the smoke slowly.

Zoe returns the greeting quietly, trying to smile. Failing. In the glow of the lamplight and behind round lenses, she meets two eyes that look at her gravely. There is something strangely familiar about him.

The song of cicadas becomes almost deafening.

"You know what I was writing?" he finally asks her.

"Of a sunset at the Valley of Desolation?"

"Of a woman in the sunset."

Involuntarily, Zoe folds an arm across her chest, feeling suddenly exposed.

She looks at his hands: big, rough like ocean shells, fingers as sturdy as branches, nails short, square and in places half broken. Hands more used to working the land or the ropes of a sailboat than to holding a pen. He is well into his forties, she assumes, not fifty yet.

"Are you a writer?"

"A thief of stories, I suppose."

She stares at him, uncomprehending.

"I steal from silence stories waiting to be told."

Zoe wrings her hands, on the defensive, as though this man could also snatch the plot of her life.

"And you search for them in the Karoo?"

"Of course not. The dryness is what helps to distil the meaning. Maybe I'm not the only one who thinks this way," he says, openly watching her reaction as he draws on his cigarette.

Zoe looks away, embarrassed, dodging the question.

"You always need places like this to write?" she asks instead, trying to avert the attention from her.

"Now that I'm allowed to spoil myself, yes."

This man seems to follow enigmatic patterns of speech.

The waitress appears on the patio, walks quickly to him and whispers something in his ear.

"You'll excuse me. I must go."

"Please," Zoe replies, dismissing him with a nod, thankful for the interruption.

Instead of leaving, as she expects, he stands there, watching her, his brow slightly furrowed.

"Meetings in the desert are never by accident," he finally says. "We might see each other again."

Perhaps it's just an impression, but suddenly she seems to read deep sadness in the stranger's eyes. Or is it just a reflection of hers?

"Who knows," she replies with a faint voice, "perhaps on another blank page ..."

The next morning, even before sunrise, Zoe is already far away, racing towards the ocean.

—4—

THE FINISTÈRE

Once she is through the Outeniqua Pass, Zoe breathes the ocean's presence in the air coming through the open window, the heather wrinkled by the wind, the clouds running large and fast like sails unfurled across the world. At last she sees it, rough and immense, stretching all the way to Antarctica: sun-scorched Africa on one shore, eternal ice on the other; two extremes facing each other across 3,300 nautical miles. "No doubt God played with geography here," Aunt Claire once said peering over her shoulder while Zoe was colouring a map of the region for a school project. "The ultimate contrast. No undertones."

A memory far in the back of her mind floods in, poignantly.

Aunt Claire's health has taken a sudden turn and Zoe has been summoned to her deathbed. She has just turned sixteen. As she enters the room, Aunt Claire gestures her to sit on the bed and takes her hand. She is breathing heavily, with great difficulty.

"My love," she says, wincing with pain, "there's something you should know about our family." She stops to look at her, her eyes now troubled and moistened. "I was just a bit older

than you when I found out what binds us firstborn females," she then goes on feebly. "Great-Aunt Charlotte, your great-grandfather's sister, had your hair colour: coppery as vine leaves in the fall. And the same jade-green eyes, I believe." She pauses and sighs. Her hands start shaking violently. "Not enough time left to tell you all I should," she rushes to say, her voice no more than a whisper.

Zoe remembers the scene so vividly now, the anxious look in her aunt's eyes as she gestured frantically towards the bedside table.

"Take these keys. Climb into the attic and look for a dark trunk hidden under some old carpets. The biggest key opens its lock. Inside, among other things, you'll find a small chest; open it with this smaller key and you'll find my diary and what's left of Great-Aunt Charlotte's diary after the fire that destroyed part of the house. Read them carefully. Those pages will tell you everything you need to know." Zoe knows what trunk Aunt Claire is talking about. She and her brother have spent many hours together in that attic, hungry for memories, for traces left by their parents.

They were a remarkable couple, as far as she can now remember. Dad—well built, with dark fiery eyes and black curls dangling over his forehead; a farmer longing for the sea, ready to set sail on his cutter whenever he could get away. Mom—slim and distant, her blond hair always tied in a perfectly shaped bun; she was English, the daughter of impoverished noble landowners, and loved horses. Zoe's father, Jean Du Plessis, had met her during a safari in what at the time was Rhodesia. He had been invited to a friend's game farm and among the guest hunters had found this splendid Amazon—fifteen years younger than him—who could ride and shoot like a man. It was 1957. Six months later they were married, with their respective families' disapproval. At least this is what Zoe was told. The Du Plessis family, in particular, didn't forgive Jean's betrayal of their *volk*. They wouldn't forget what the British had done fifty years earlier during the Anglo-Boer War, when thousands of Afrikaner women and children had been left to die in Queen Victoria's concentration camps.

Be that as it may, Gloria followed her husband to the Cape. However, it didn't take long for this daughter of the British Empire to regret such boldness. Other than her love for horse racing, she had landed in the wrong place to socialize. Pretty soon she got as tired of the hunting trips as of the evening parties that Jean arranged for her in the great hall of the Finistère, the estate his dying father had eventually bequeathed to him, his only male heir, a year after their marriage.

Zoe grew up with the image of this blonde sylph wrapped in long silk dresses, busy entertaining guests in the glow of candles, a glass of champagne in hand, her lips a condescending half smile. This was Gloria: young, charming, and unsatisfied. Only many years later Zoe would find out from an old family friend that her mother cheated on her husband, and that the car accident that instantly killed both her parents took place after the two, drunk with rage and Martini cocktails, left a party fighting about Gloria's love affairs.

Now that she thinks of it, all along Zoe has been attracted to women who look superbly sophisticated in their slim bodies, delicate traits, pale complexions—their deceitful frailness reminding her of her mother and highlighting, by contrast, how she differs from her. With her bulky breasts, sunburnt skin and muscular shoulders, she has nothing of Gloria's seductiveness, nothing of the English huntress with whom her father fell madly in love.

"The virgin of the fossils." This is what her colleagues call her instead. When she once inquired about it, Piet made a half-joke out of pure embarrassment, revealing a personal sore spot: "C'mon Zoe, it seems far easier for you to give yourself to an *Australopithecus* than to a man in the flesh." She is not that impervious to the other sex, she has always believed. In retrospect, however, although she looked at them with the scepticism of a scientist, her aunts' diaries did leave a mark on her. Her subconscious, she now realizes, acted as a potent inhibitor in her love relationships: The moment they turned emotionally demanding, she would walk away. Only Dario succeeded in breaking her subliminal veto. Now she has to face its dire consequences.

Once again, the vision of Aunt Claire's deathbed resurfaces from the half-buried past.

Her aunt's voice has grown softer and softer. She often pauses to suck air with an effort, her chest squashed by an invisible boulder. "Your life will be hard. You'll have to be strong … At least, I had you and André to look after … You children were my salvation," she mutters as Zoe dabs at beads of sweat on her forehead with a cloth. "Don't be afraid to go it alone, though. Find a purpose worthy of being pursued with utmost dedication. Don't waste your life. Don't make Charlotte's mistake!"

Exhausted, Aunt Claire closes her eyes. Her hands are now resting on the linen sheet as inert roots. When her last words come they are barely audible yet strike Zoe with their intensity: "Never reveal what you'll find in those diaries. I beg you!" Her aunt's eyes, suddenly wide open, are fixed into hers. Shaken, Zoe nods. Two hours later, Aunt Claire takes her last breath. At her behest, Willem Heyns, the estate's director, is appointed as guardian of the two young Du Plessis children, until Zoe comes of age.

The fuel gauge light starts blinking, drawing Zoe away from her recollections. She straightens her back against the car seat and sets her gaze upon the last chain of mountains before the Finistère. Fifty kilometres later, she rolls the car down the other side of the Franschhoek Pass towards an undulating sea of vineyards. After the dryness of the Karoo, the valley seems ever greener. It shines proud and confident under a sky like cobalt blue porcelain. In the flawless light, the red spikes of flamboyant trees and the snow-white gables of the Cape Dutch farmhouses seem to come directly at the eye. It's an optical effect that verges on the sense of touch.

As she pulls into the driveway of the Finistère lined with tall camphor trees, Zoe slows down, taking in its centuries-old spirit. With time she has come to regard this last stretch of road as part of a cleansing ritual. Going through this leafy tunnel means purging oneself of the evils and worries of the outside world. Emerging from its shadows, she blinks at the glare of the white-washed façade of the Finistère. She is home. But, this time, she is not cleansed.

❁❁❁

Zoe's still getting her bag out of the car when she hears the sound of hurried footsteps on the gravel. She turns and finds herself in the fat, golden brown arms of Georgina, the old housekeeper. After their aunt's death, she is the one who raised her and her brother to the rhythm of the harvests. Everything seems to overflow ever so gently from her: her generous disposition, her wide hips, her muscular legs, her breasts—swollen like ripe grapefruits and soft as home-made butter. There is always something warm and reassuring in her physical contact. For a moment, Georgina's smile emphasizes a row of large white regular teeth, before she closes her mouth abruptly, staring at Zoe in disbelief.

"My baby! What have you done to your hair?"

"Just wanted to try something different."

Instead of grinning at her quip, Zoe looks sadly into her *aia*'s eyes and then buries her face in the tangle of her frizzy grey hair. She smells ginger.

"André told me you'd come today. He's out with the men right now. I'll send someone to let him know you are here."

"No, wait. I'd rather go. Where?"

"Over there." Georgina points towards that part of the vineyard that clambers more steeply up the flank of the hill. Zoe walks into it, gazing at the rows of wavy green hills crashing against a crown of purple mountains. She spots her brother and old Willem busy checking young vines. As she walks towards them she takes in André's features, so starkly Mediterranean, as if his face had been carved wildly—the irregular nose, the nervous mouth, the prominent cheekbones—or had been drawn in charcoal—black eyes, dark locks of unkempt hair.

He looks more and more like dad. Only his skin colour,

even though belonging to someone used to living out of doors, reveals traces of a diaphanous English pallor. He wears an old chequered shirt and khaki pants; Zoe reckons he must have put on some weight since the last time they saw each other. When André spots her, he runs up, presses her to him with one arm and, with his free hand, rubs her skull in what is a habitual gesture of affection between them.

"Redhead! You're back at last! What happened to your mane, though? I hardly recognize you."

"Not you too, André. Georgina has already told me off."

He releases her so that she can greet Willem. Zoe extends her hand. Despite his age—the director of the Finistère is now well over sixty—his grip is firm as ever. As usual, when they meet there is coldness in their greeting.

Her brother proudly motions towards the new buds.

"Come and see our new vines. We're trying to grow good Chardonnay on this side of the hill. It will take no fewer than five years."

"Quite some time," she says without really paying attention.

"Not for those who work with vineyards," Willem says.

Zoe looks at the director unblinking. Instead of replying she turns to her brother: "Shall we head home, André?"

As they walk towards the house, he no longer holds it back: "You're a mess *ousus*, no kidding. Has your Latin Lover anything to do with it?"

"Dario died. Three days ago. A hijacking."

André tightly wraps his arm under her shoulder and keeps walking, without saying a word. Silence is his way of expressing sorrow, pain, grief.

A childhood memory flashes back. Zoe doesn't censor it.

A policewoman informs them of the death of their parents. André sits speechless, staring at the lady in uniform, then runs up the stairs and takes refuge in the attic. For five days he locks himself up there. Zoe brings him baskets with food prepared by Georgina. He doesn't even bother looking at her. Eventually, though, they take to eating together, holed up in their lonely nest, away from everything and everyone. Day after day, lying on frayed Oriental rugs, through the small attic window they watch the light fade away in the treetops. At night, André curls up next to her like a blind kitten in search of warmth. Zoe keeps him close to her, humming the old lullabies their aia *taught them. No one interferes with their grieving. The Finistère waits, hoping that, in a few weeks, a nine-year-old boy would turn into a man.*

"Were you serious about him?" André finally asks.

Zoe leans on his shoulder.

"*Ja*."

With his arm now around her waist, André leads her towards the jacaranda behind the big house; so many times have they played, fought, cried, laughed together under its canopy. They sit in its green shadow, letting their fraternal warmth join forces with the reassuring steadiness of the tree.

❁❁❁

It's dusk when they walk into Georgina's kitchen. On the large wooden table, stacked neatly in rows of four, are dozens of *gemmerkoekies*.

"You rarely come to see us these days. And look at how skinny you are!" Georgina says, feeling her waist with chubby fingers. "When is the last time you ate a proper *bobotie*?"

Zoe grabs a biscuit. She is hungry, despite it all. She bites into the gingery soul of the cookie.

"They taste as good as ever, *Ouma*."

Meanwhile, André pours two cups of coffee from the hot pot on the stove and sits at the large square table; it's so big that in their youth more than once she and her brother danced on it. Since the day they were orphaned and against Willem's will, they've taken all their meals in the kitchen rather than in the severe dining room. Their friends too, when they came for a visit, would prefer the cozy warmth of Georgina's world, with its copper pots and pans hanging on the wall, the huge old wood-burning oven always lit in winter, the jars of jams and preserves neatly arranged on walnut shelves. On the table soon appear pancakes, toasted bread, scrambled eggs and *boerewors*. Zoe looks at their *aia* gratefully, trying not to show her sadness.

After dinner brother and sister move out on the covered *stoep*. Zoe sinks into a low wicker chair and closes her eyes, breathing in the scent of jasmine in bloom.

"How long will you stay?"

"A week. I fly back on Wednesday morning."

"So soon? Can't you take a few more days off work? It won't be easy for you back there."

"I know."

André waits for his sister's thoughts to wander through the silence of the night.

"I will ask Kuyper to send me into the bush," she says at last.

"Where?"

"In the Kalahari."

"Another desert."

A full moon is rising across the valley from behind the darkened mountains.

"Africa kills, Africa resurrects," dad used to say. "Perhaps up there you will find some relief."

Zoe doesn't reply. She knows she won't—she is a first-born Du Plessis.

André draws closer and gently passes his hand through her cropped hair.

"You're exhausted. Have a good sleep and let the Finistère take care of you."

— 5 —

FAMILY SECRETS

HER ROOM IS unchanged. The adventure novels, the atlases, the scientific texts: Everything is in its usual place, as if this were the museum of her own life. Shells, rocks, minerals, bird feathers, collections of beetles and butterflies in small glass cases fill the shelves. Each object she gazes upon has a story to tell. On the mantelpiece, two human skulls still catch the eye: Zoe was about thirteen when she decided to place them there.

Her mind goes back to that evening when, walking in to wish her good night, her mother found those four empty sockets staring at her.

She is not impressed. "How did you get them?" she asks in that annoyingly dry tone of hers. Zoe is reluctant to reveal that dad has procured the skulls at her request. She had spotted them in an antique shop in Cape Town while waiting for her mum, busy with some last-minute errands. She knows the issue might be yet another source of discord between her parents. When she had asked for the skulls on the spot, Gloria had refused to buy them. Now, after tortuous negotiations, she surrenders and allows her to keep those gruesome remains where they are. Since that night, however, Zoe senses her mum no longer feels comfortable entering the room of this unruly and introverted daughter of hers, seemingly more in love with the dead than with the living.

Twenty years later, Zoe wonders if this was her little revenge for having felt excluded from her mother's fatuous and glistening world.

She undresses and puts on an old linen nightgown, breathing in the faint trace of lavender. She looks at the heavy oak cabinet in front of her, hesitates, then opens it and removes a pile of blankets to free the box she recovered at the time of Aunt Claire's death. She pauses to look at it, lightly touching its simple shape, imagining the hand that crafted it: all that patient file and sandpaper work to smooth edges, trying to infuse a touch of discreet gentleness amidst the harshness of frontier life.

She walks to the mantelpiece and shoves a finger into the eye socket of one of the skulls to retrieve a small key hidden inside.

As she opens the box, her mind races back to the night when she ventured into the attic looking for the diaries. She relives the sense of anticipation once she found those well-guarded written memories and started reading them, but also the mixed feeling of gruesome fascination and disappointment as she went through records which dripped with family drama and outmoded lyricism. Because, in the end, what she discovered in those pages seemed to her the workings of altered minds, at times steeped in horror, more than the recounting of factual stories. In any case, all that —she told herself at that time—had nothing to do with her. With Dario's death, however, the narrative engraved in those pages has suddenly acquired a stark, albeit irrational, authenticity.

Fighting her exhaustion, Zoe pages through the journal of Great-Aunt Charlotte, the sister of her great-grandfather. She hasn't opened it since that night, eighteen years ago. Now, after what has just happened, she feels the urge to go back to it and read it under a different light. The notebook is made of thick yellow paper covered with worn leather and secured shut by a lace wrapped several times around it. Unfortunately, two-fifths of it has been reduced to ashes. Its pages break off abruptly, sinking into scorched edges, so that often one has to guess what the surviving stubs of words might mean.

The diary begins with the family tree and the history of the Du Plessis family. Evidently, the line of descent was copied from the final pages, left blank on purpose, of the voluminous Bible that Jean-Marc Du Plessis brought with him from Holland. Often regarded as the only real asset by most pioneer families, that old tome weighing several pounds passed intact from one generation to another—till hers. Year after year, every death, birth or marriage was scrupulously recorded in there. Zoe runs her finger through the tree branches and stops at Charlotte's name. She was a first-born, like her.

The journal's historical account starts in 1698, the year in which Jean-Marc Du Plessis landed in Cape Town with his wife and two sons, along with another hundred and eighty French Huguenots. They were all fleeing the wave of repression unleashed in France against the Reformed, as the followers of Calvin's doctrine called themselves. Many escaped from certain death by taking refuge in Amsterdam, at the time the cradle of Protestantism. A handful of them ended up boarding a ship of the Dutch East India Company and trying their luck in the Cape Colony. Each family had been promised a plot of arable land. In this fashion, the French vignerons' knowledge and skills reached the southern tip of Africa. It was their Calvinist faith, coupled with their religious zeal, that forever united Huguenots and Boers in their African destiny.

Zoe leafs through the journal, trying to find a specific passage. She recognizes it immediately: The handwriting is uncertain and fragmented, as if the author had been in the grip of strong emotion. Moreover, in that spot the paper is unusually wrinkled. She is sure this page contains Aunt Charlotte's desiccated tears.

Franschhoek, November 13, 1899

For as long as I will live, I will not go through a more painful day. For us settlers, life here in Africa has never been a light ride. But what I have learned today goes beyond the most horrific act of the imagination. I don't know why I'm writing this, perhaps just to keep at bay this unbearable pain.

Today Frank Russell, my fiancé, died falling from his horse during a race. He was twenty-seven and I loved him to distraction. He was my sun, my air, my music. My talking about him in the past seems so absurd! So far, I hadn't written anything about him. I was afraid someone might read my journal before we made our engagement official. Now I could fill whole pages about our secret meetings, our walks in the moonlight, our early-morning rides on the river bank.

> *Frank died, and with him died the woman in me. I will slowly wither, preserving my family honour. If he could, Frank would offer me the whole world, balancing it on the tip of an ostrich feather. He did much more than that, he gave me his life. Last night he asked Dad for my hand. And father said yes. We would be married in autumn, right after the harvest. My happiness lasted less than twenty-four hours. My anger and my guilt will last forever. For Frank's death was not an accident, it was already written in my destiny. This whole story of the Du Plessis' curse had always sounded so far-fetched to me. But facts rubbed the truth in my face, wiping off any doubt.*

Zoe gently closes the journal and lets her ancestor's anguish join hers. Their shameful secret is now weighing on her heart too. Everything is quiet in the house; only the barking of a solitary dog comes from far away. Zoe turns out the light. In the semi-darkness, she sees the moon's rays create patches of milky light on her coverlet. But she now hates the magic of this moment and buries her head under the pillow, wishing only for a dreamless sleep.

— 6 —
THE BLACK PARTNER

For the next four days, Zoe doesn't do much except walk through the vineyards and, in the hottest hours of the day, sit in her bedroom to re-read Aunt Charlotte's journal. She is locked in her mourning and André makes sure nothing interferes with the cocoon into which she has retreated. Only the sound of farm activities comes to her like an unpleasant reminder that life still goes on. She usually meets her brother just before sunset, to have tea together on the *stoep* and watch the sun take its leave behind a blue strip of mountains.

"Willem is getting old, it's time for him to enjoy his retirement years," André says one evening sucking avidly at his Gitanes cigarette, as if smoke could protect him from the coldness of this statement.

The news comes as a relief—at least for her—but her brother looks troubled. The director of the Finistère occupies a major role, Zoe knows that. Not only must he manage the workers and their families, but he is also the one entrusted with the quality control of grapes and the whole production line. André, as their father and grandfather did before him, is mainly involved in sales and distribution.

"The amount of work has increased, recently," André

says. "With the end of the boycott, we have started selling our Cape wines in Europe and the States."

"Then you need someone with a good and clear idea of the market out there," Zoe says pouring tea into their cups.

"Definitely."

"Have you already a replacement in mind?" she asks rather absent-mindedly, her eyes half-closed.

"Actually, yes. Although I wanted to discuss the matter with you first. I'd like your take on this."

"Since when do you need to consult with me to make decisions about the farm?"

"This time it's different," André replies, lowering his voice. "I want to replace him with a black man."

Involuntarily, Zoe stops stirring honey in her tea. The tinkling of the teaspoon fades away, leaving behind a revealing silence. She turns to face him. He holds her gaze. She knows him too well: This time he is not kidding.

"You should see your face!" he exclaims, relaxing his mouth in a half smile. "Wasn't it you who once even told me off for being too harsh with our black workers?"

"You're right. You left me speechless."

Examining her reaction, Zoe has to admit that forty years of apartheid have taken their toll—even on her. She has always been in favour of black empowerment; redistribution is long overdue. Fifteen per cent of Whites should no longer control ninety percent of the country's economy. Now that the matter concerns them directly, though, she can't hide her hesitancy to face such a drastic change.

"Tell me about him, then."

"His name is Cyril Kunene; he's thirty-eight, a Xhosa. He graduated in viticulture thanks to a scholarship offered by an American university. He then entered the wine business and became a buyer. Today, his company handles much of the import of South African wines to the United States. That's it, in short."

"A strong C.V., no doubt," Zoe says watching Georgina bring in quilts and coverlets after having aired them. "What's his name again?"

"Cyril. Cyril Kunene."

"From what I can infer Mr. Kunene knows viticulture as well as the marketing side of things?"

"Right after graduating he worked in wineries in California."

"Is he already working for us?"

"Not yet. He's a consultant at Mont Rochelle."

"But they're our competitors!"

"We've had a couple of secret meetings. He'd be willing to join us."

Zoe looks André straight in the eye: "Yet, you're not entirely convinced."

"There's something else."

"What else?"

"He's asking for a percentage of profits."

"How much?"

"Twenty percent."

"Would you agree?"

André lets the question linger in the air as she sips her tea.

"I feel we should accept," he eventually says. "His presence would guarantee us greater exposure to the US market. I've been thinking a lot about it, lately. A black director might also attract media attention and have a positive effect, market-wise."

"Are you telling me you're buying his image?" It's the first time she sees her brother in this light: a clever entrepreneur turned into a shrewd opportunist.

"Of course," André replies, "he knows very well what he's worth right now."

"And how is he as a person? As much a schemer as you seem to be?"

Zoe notices André's jaw tense slightly; then, bending his head to the side, he grins at her.

"I'm not that cynical, *ousus*. I like Cyril. He's straightforward, intelligent and knowledgeable. I think it would be nice working with him. Willem and I have never really clicked. Lately, we seem to disagree pretty much about everything."

"Did you tell him about Kunene?"

"Of course not."

"He would see you as another renegade eager to melt into the new Rainbow Nation," she says with a sneer.

"Miserable *hensoppers*," André croaks mimicking Willem's parlance. To this day, many Boers regard as cowards those who during the Anglo-Boer War accepted defeat and surrendered. As much as the *bittereinders*, those who resisted till the "bitter end" preferring death to dishonour, are commended for their heroism.

Zoe smiles at her brother, basking in their sarcastic camaraderie.

"The British didn't manage to wipe us out, nor will the niggers," she says, mimicking Willem herself. Then, after a pause, she adds: "He's wrong. We'll be gone ... and the sooner, the better."

André looks at her, his tongue suddenly dry. She immediately regrets having spoken so plainly. Even more than her words, it's the harshness in her voice that has struck him. She can see it in his eyes.

"You might have a point there," he says. "We are destined to become a cumbersome minority. As you can see, I've taken note too. Either we reinvent ourselves, or we end up gathering dust in the cellar. Cyril might offer us that touch of *exotic* novelty required by changed circumstances." He utters that word—exotic—letting sarcasm do its dirty job.

"You seem to have made up your mind," Zoe says, not missing the fact that her brother already calls their future black partner by his first name.

"*Nee*, I haven't. You have the final say. I trust your instincts. I'll make sure you meet him before you leave."

But she has already decided. It will be a "yes." No doubt about it.

By suggesting a brilliant black man might join the family enterprise, André has involuntarily evoked from her past the ghost of Thabo Nyathi. A South African by origin, Thabo had moved to England thanks to a scholarship that allowed him to bypass the Bantu Education system, which prevented Blacks from attending white universities. After graduating with flying colours, in the mid-1980s he attended a special course in London where he met Zoe.

At the time, Professor Johan Kuyper was in the process of launching a new research unit at the Witwatersrand University and needed young, promising scholars. They both applied for a position there. The choice fell on her—a Du Plessis—and Piet de Vries, another thoroughbred Afrikaner. Thabo, the best among the candidates, didn't make it. He accepted the verdict with composed dignity. She accepted the posting without venturing to say a word in his favour. They both knew Thabo would be precluded from any further career in the field of paleoanthropology, at least in South Africa.

At that time, not even academia, supposedly the patron of broad-mindedness, was ready to open its doors to Blacks. But even out there in the bigger world, Zoe asked herself then, conscious of this injustice: How many black paleoanthropologists were there? Did they exist? Did they have a voice? Did they publish books? Although the largest number of hominid fossils had been found in Africa, she was not aware of any paleoanthropological research team headed by a black. As in the golden age of safaris, the white *bwana* commanded and the black porter looked after the luggage.

She hasn't heard from Thabo since then. But she has never forgiven herself for having kept quiet. The moral wrong has seeped into her, day after day, digging into her. To no one has she confessed her cowardice. For years she has felt this infamy burn inside her. She's no better than other Whites who, being in the know, kept their mouths shut; who, at seeing a black kicked or whipped with the *sjambok*, have turned their head away. This sick feeling about herself has grown within her like a consuming cancer—it clogs the pores, deadens the heart. André too may be burning with the same shame. By opening the door to a black partner, he is perhaps trying to free his soul.

—7—
THE CURSE

"DO YOU MISS him?"

Her brother moves closer while she is leaning against the door frame, on the *stoep*, and begins massaging her neck and shoulders, stiffened by sleepless nights. Zoe lets her gaze wander over the estate vineyards, which shine motionless in the moon's milky embrace. Since her arrival, André has never mentioned Dario and she is grateful for that. She answers in a whisper, more to herself than to him.

"Badly."

It's her next-to-last night at the Finistère. The idea of leaving this place frightens her. Another forty-eight hours and she'll have to face life again.

"Stay," André says, sensing her wavering.

Why? Just to keep on pretending nothing happened?

She lets silence answer for her as it gently descends on them and the night.

Later, alone in her room, she opens Charlotte's diary again. She has already read the first half, in which her great-aunt, relying upon the oral accounts of the older members of her family, put together their family history and the founding of the Finistère. In her endeavour she tried to be as accurate as possible. Somehow, despite the roughness and the simple needs of pioneering life, Charlotte developed the sensitivity of a historian and poet. The chronicle begins with the arduous sixty-kilometre crossing via ox-wagon that brought Jean-Marc Du Plessis and his family from Cape Town to what was then called Olifants Hoek, the Elephants' Corner.

> *The cartwheels of the Huguenots followed the same old path opened by generations of pachyderms across the mountainous interior and into a valley which, in the eyes of those early pioneers, looked like a gift from God: vast and lush, designed by the winding course of a great river, protected on both sides by a tall mountain ridge. Soon the settlement changed its name and became known as Franschhoek, the French Corner. The plot of land that the Company allocated to Jean-Marc Du Plessis ran from the foothills down into the valley until it reached the banks of the Berg River. It was south-facing, protected from the Atlantic winds and particularly well suited to receive the two hundred vines that our ancestor had transported, miraculously intact, across an ocean. Jean-Marc Du Plessis decided to build his homestead half-way down the slope, so as to dominate the vineyards below. Initially, he settled for a simple, rectangular one-storey structure with thatched roofs and white-washed walls. Only later would he and his sons add a second floor, the side wings, the elaborately ornate gable and the covered stoep, with its classical columns and benches covered in blue Delft tiles. The name, however, would remain unchanged. When he*

> *landed in the Cape, our ancestor thought he had reached the end of the world—the end of the civilized world, at least. No wonder he named the farm thinking of the Finistère, the extreme west of Brittany's coastline where the Atlantic opens up in its disturbing immensity. Finistère, from the Latin* finis terrae*—our* predikant *told me once—that is, land's end.*

Zoe stops reading and lets her thoughts wander. The marine curve of the horizon has always inspired a desire for freedom and adventure: It's the spirit of the open sea, its invitation to discover what lies beyond.

Many set sail from that Breton coast: pirates, adventurers, merchants, explorers. All, more or less, magnetically attracted by *l'ailleur*—the elsewhere. A French Calvinist on the run, Jean-Marc fled France and its Finistère only to find, on another Atlantic coast, a new Finistère. Those who leave, always return: if not to the same place, at least to the memory of it.

Zoe looks one more time out of the window into the darkness, chasing her thoughts. Then she resumes her reading.

> *Almost two centuries have gone by since our ancestor died longing for his French vineyards, and I have come to see things very differently. My roots are here, in this land. For Jean-Marc, his true Finistère, the land of the heart, lay in Brittany; for me, it is here, in this valley suspended at the remote tip of another continent. The British frown upon our wish to belong to Africa, but I am proud to call myself Afrikaner.*

The journal is filled with such considerations. More than once Zoe marvels at the depth of reasoning of her ancestor—after all, she was just a humble, late nineteenth-century countrywoman. Yet, the scorched pages are there. She lingers a moment again, but when her eyes go back to her aunt's writing, Zoe feels the blood pounding in her veins, her hands getting moist. She is reaching the entries that most trouble her.

Franschhoek, January 15, 1897

Today Aunt Adèle, grandfather's sister, my great-aunt, told me something that, frankly, I can hardly believe. I have always considered her an easily impressionable woman. And bigoted too. However, today she has provided me with a different interpretation of her celibacy. "Dear Charlotte," she said, "next month you will be eighteen and it's about time you were made aware of the pitiful fate that unites us." As an explanation to, I guess, my visibly shocked expression, she rushed to add: "You too, like me, are a first-born female of the Du Plessis family." Still, I had no clue.

Before saying anything else, though, she made me swear not to tell a word of what she was about to reveal: it would ruin our family. I had never seen her so gravely concerned. Thus, I promised.

Her story-telling started with what her own aunt Desirée, the older sister of my great-grandfather, told her at her deathbed. She just added some bits and pieces when needed, to give me the whole picture. From what I gathered, towards the end of the eighteenth century some members of our family left the Finistère to go into the interior, following the caravans of the Trekboere *headed to the North East. They had had enough of the restrictions imposed by the Company and wanted to break free. Among them was my great-great-grandfather Gustave, then twenty years old.*

It was a long trek, treacherous and exhausting and Aunt Adèle was keen to provide all the details about it. Several times the Trekboere *were forced to disassemble the wagons and transport them on their shoulders across the most challenging mountain passes. After months of trekking, they finally reached a fertile valley marked by the course of the Great Fish River. Gustave—in the meantime he had married Gretel, the caravan head's daughter—and the other Boer families thought this was a good place to build their homesteads. "Little did they know," Aunt Adèle said in commenting on this bit of the story. She then explained how the Xhosa, nomadic herders coming from the lands north of the Zambezi River, had also set their eyes on those prairies. In the beginning, both tribes managed to keep a safe distance from each other. But then frictions started to surface, until they turned into open clashes. Boer farmers attacked and were in turn attacked; often they were forced to barricade themselves in their homesteads, while the Xhosa raided their cattle. During one of these raids, Gretel, Gustave's wife, was stabbed in the throat by a spear while she reloaded his gun.*

Mad with rage and grief, Gustave and his commando attacked a Xhosa village slaughtering anyone in their path: old men, women, children. They were about to get away after having set fire to several mud huts when Gustave found his way barred by an old woman wearing a strange headdress. Here I think Aunt Adèle—or was it Aunt Desirée's fault?—let her imagination run a bit too wild. She vividly described the old woman, covered in blood, how she met Gustave's eyes as she raised and frantically waved a stick in her left hand, shouting something at him. It was the 23rd of October 1801. Back at the farm, Gustave asked his Khoikhoi slave Noma, who had witnessed the scene and knew the language of the Xhosa, what the old woman had yelled at him. The slave explained that the old woman was an amagqira, *a diviner, and that he wouldn't repeat her words: They contained a terrible curse. Gustave raised his* sjambok *and Noma had to give in. Here is his translation in Afrikaans: "White Man! From now on, the firstborn females in your family will see their men die before producing offspring. May you all be damned, forever!"*

Gustave returned to the Finistère only many years later, and only then did he find out that the husband of his sister Desirée had drowned in the river when she was in the fourth month of her first pregnancy. Shock and grief had made her lose the baby. Troubled by that account, Gustave asked her the exact date and time of when the accident had happened. Desirée complied, slightly puzzled by that question. The date was the 23rd of October of the year 1801, late in the afternoon.

His sister never interrupted him when Gustave told her about his commando's retaliation raid against the Xhosa village, the blood, the amagqira's *curse, the old woman's eyes full of hatred and revenge. "I ruined*

> *your life," he finally said. Two days later, he shot himself. Desirée never remarried.*
>
> *"I too will die a lonely woman," Aunt Adèle said. I tried to talk some sense into her. I thought it was madness and it probably showed on my face. How could she believe such a thing? No doubt, it was all very tragic, but it might have been a fatal coincidence. "At first, I couldn't believe it either," aunt said, on the verge of crying. "Perhaps if I tell you my own story as well, you'll understand."*
>
> *It was getting late, though; the candle was dying and she looked exhausted. So, she sent me to bed. I'll have to wait till tomorrow to hear her story.*

Zoe puts out the light, following mentally the gesture that Aunt Charlotte would make to extinguish the candle before sliding under her quilt. She feels very close to her. Her diary entries are brimming with enthusiasm, love of life, youthful hopes; they reveal the first awkward attempts to challenge the strict social rules imposed by the faith of their fathers. Foolishly, perhaps, she feels for this late nineteenth-century girl, with long plaits coiled on either side of her head, meekly looking at her from the family photo album.

— 8 —

UNDER THE BIG OAK TREE

THE NEXT MORNING, as Zoe is having breakfast in Georgina's kitchen, her brother storms in, takes a couple of *koekies* from her plate and rushes to pour himself a cup of coffee. There's an unusual excitement in his eyes; for the first time since her arrival, he is trying to break through the desolate composure within which she has confined herself.

"*Kom ousus*, hurry up!" He gestures as if he wanted to drag her from her chair.

"Where to?"

"Cyril Kunene. He's waiting for us under the big oak tree, by the river."

She looks away, while André sips his coffee. She's not in the mood to meet anyone—let alone Kunene. She's not ready to leave the sheltered cocoon of her apathy; all she feels like doing is crawling back into her bedroom. Yet, she can't let her brother down. In all these years, he has never asked for her help with the farm. She owes him.

André looks up from his cup and says, almost in a whisper: "Jolly's already saddled."

She keeps silent, still uncertain. André turns his back to refill his cup, lowering his head over the pot, as if in prayer.

She watches the nape of his neck now laid bare, totally vulnerable.

In a flash, she springs from her chair and darts out of the kitchen, into the courtyard. Two horses are waiting there, as she has expected. Jolly, her mare, snorts when she recognizes her. Out of the corner of her eye, Zoe sees that André is already at her heels. How many times did they rehearse this same scene in their youth?

She finds herself grimacing as she quickly tightens the girth strap. Then she jumps on the horse's back and rushes down the hill, along the passage that opens between the grapes. Her stirrups, she notices, are at the right length. She is holding Jolly, giving her little rein; but the mare knows that the moment they reach the bottom of the hill her mistress will let her loose. At that point, Zoe tightens her knees against Jolly's sides and the horse breaks into a wild gallop. Zoe glances over her shoulder and sees André leaning over his steed, urging it faster. They're down the valley, now, across the field leading to the oak tree. André is gaining ground. She feels her untrained leg muscles giving way and making her lose balance; she races the last few hundred metres clinging with one hand to the horse's mane. It's an undignified victory; most of all, it's a victory that leaves a bitter aftertaste in her mouth.

❁❁❁

Under the oak tree, visibly amused, a young man in a steel-grey, freshly pressed business suit has followed the race.

"I bet on the right horse," he cries as he takes Zoe's reins, holds her leg and skilfully helps her to dismount.

"Thanks."

"Don't mention it," he answers in a polished English accent.

Zoe turns her head in time to catch André's childish, annoyed expression.

"You cheated, as always."

Her brother quickly dismounts, the light of mockery still in his eyes. Then, turning to the man in the grey suit: "Zoe, let me introduce you to Cyril Kunene. Cyril, this is my sister, Zoe Du Plessis."

Mr. Kunene—to her he is not Cyril, yet—shakes her hand formally, looking straight into her eyes. The tall black gentleman standing in front of her shows the lean and self-assured look of a New Yorker accustomed to doing business in the city. He belongs in another league, she senses, as she takes in his features: soft, full lips, high cheekbones, beautifully shaped almond eyes slightly turning downward—indeed, a perfect poster man for the post-apartheid era.

They sit around a wooden plank in the oak tree's shade.

Kunene takes out a bottle and three glasses from a cooler handbag.

"I thought you might be interested in tasting our new Merlot, aged in Nevers oak barrels."

He uncorks the bottle, briefly sniffs the cork, pours a small taste in his glass and checks the wine before pouring it into their glasses, starting with Zoe's. Despite being the descendant of nine generations of winemakers, she doesn't consider herself a connoisseur. At all. Thus, she leaves it to her brother, who's already sniffing the wine and checking its colour before taking a liberal sip to get the wine's mouthfeel. André swallows and waits for the aftertaste to kick in before expressing his approval: "It has a lovely character, soft and velvety. Perhaps that trace of wild fruit that makes our wines unique is a bit too pronounced here. It's still young, but quite promising."

"*Goed*," Cyril says, switching to Afrikaans. He too breathes in the southern fragrance from his glass, his eyes flashing proudly. "What about you, *Mejuffrow* Du Plessis?"

She looks at him slightly disconcerted. The change of language hasn't gone unnoticed, nor has the subtle statement it implies. Cyril doesn't mind using a language he might despise if it helps to create a bridge between them, a space of familiarity. *Yet, how ironic.* A Black chooses to speak Afrikaans, the language of the former oppressor, while we Afrikaners are purposefully erasing it from our lives, ashamed to reveal what our blood sounds like. She hasn't forgotten the pang of embarrassment she felt when Dario once asked her: "How come you never speak Afrikaans with your people in public?"

She got herself off the hook, back then, with a pleasantry so out of her character: "Darling, since you don't understand it, it wouldn't be polite." When in fact she would have had to admit she too was tacitly responding to the pressing need of changing skins on the run.

The prospective partner graciously gestures at Zoe's glass, bringing her attention back to it: "So?"

"I'm not an expert like you two ..." she replies in a hushed voice, as it often happens to her when she feels, even briefly, the centre of attention. As she speaks, Zoe meets her brother's anxious expression. *How he longs for my approval.* Thus, she improvises. "But I confess I have a soft spot for Merlot. In this one, in particular, I recognize those notes that are dearest to me—the smells of the French countryside in autumn; the scents of distant things, perhaps lost forever."

"I admire people who can read poetry in a sip of wine," Cyril says, straightening his back. "A rare bunch, on the verge of extinction." Embarrassed, Zoe lowers her head and looks at her fingers tightly clasping the glass stem. Kunene senses her uneasiness and quickly changes the subject, turning to André. He makes some general remarks about the international wine market and chats casually with her brother about his experience with Californian grape growers. Then, almost inadvertently, he leads Zoe to talk about her research work at the Witwatersrand University, as if vines, wines and fossils had always been intimately related.

Zoe notices Kunene's natural ability in reading people. He shows a self-confidence, a natural ease in connecting with his interlocutor and exploring unfamiliar emotional territories that are unimaginable to her. He speaks slowly, distinctly enunciating each word, his hands spread on the table, his fingers perfectly manicured. She takes it all in: his ultra-thin, square-cased Vacheron Constantin wristwatch, his single-breasted tailored suit, the monogram embroidered on his shirt pocket. She hasn't seen his shoes yet. She doesn't resist the temptation and takes a quick look at his feet. There they are, a pair of handmade, black leather oxfords, polished and worn just enough not to look too new. Kunene intercepts her look.

"I don't blame you, *Mejuffrow.* Dressed as I am, you might think I'm slightly out of place here in rural Africa, in the middle of a vineyard, under an oak tree."

"Well ..." she mumbles.

"I assure you I'd feel much more comfortable wearing my jeans and a T-shirt, as you do. But let's be honest. We didn't meet here just to have a friendly conversation over a reasonably good glass of wine. We're here to talk business."

Zoe turns her head slightly to check her brother's reaction. André keeps looking into his glass; only a slight sheen of perspiration on his upper lip betrays some hidden tension. Kunene's voice lowers while he lays his honour bare at her feet.

"I'm never allowed to forget I'm black, least of all here in South Africa. Dressing up has become part and parcel of my business card. I'm sure you know what I mean."

Struck by the frankness of his confession, Zoe forces herself to keep her eyes on his, prodding him to go on.

"If I had shown up in casual attire, you'd have seen in me none other than another common black, one of those thousand 'garden boys' who patiently water plants and continue to be called 'boys' by their white *baas*. They never become 'men,' even when they're well into their seventies."

He is so very right. Cyril Kunene can't hide behind anything, neither an Ivy League degree, nor an honourable career, nor a posh uptown apartment. His skin colour stands before everything else, even when it's covered in an Armani suit. Although unsettling, he has finally played the one card left in his hand: his frankness. Why then doesn't she openly acknowledge his good reasons? What's holding her back?

"Well, let's talk business then," she says facing both men, lifting her chin a little higher. "Have you two taken into account how the other farmers in the valley will react to the ... novelty?" She is trampling on unknown ground here. "They might not like it, even boycott you ..."

"Yes, we did," her brother answers a bit too hurriedly. "While you were busy with your fossils, you may not have noticed, but things have been changing pretty fast. Our move is less risky than you might think."

She nods, and from that moment on she lets her brother manage the conversation. Again, she has the subtle feeling that the two men have known each other for some time now and that this little act has been staged just for her. Nor can she dismiss the impression of having landed in this grape field after having travelled through some sort of wormhole. As if her role could only be that of the outlier, watching from a distance as people go by their lives, or that of an intruder, prying into people's lives in search of secrets, of hidden bones.

Zoe chimes in on the men's conversation only on a couple of occasions, asking for clarifications. She finds Kunene intelligent, canny, coldly professional, and she resents him for this, for he represents the West's renewed encroachment — this time Wall Street-style — on Africa. "After all, what chances did you Boers ever give us?" he might well retort. Fair enough. Blacks will seek compensation and renewal through the dominant U.S. culture, the one now dictating economic policies to the world. Perhaps, this is how Kunene wants her to see him, while instead inside him there still lies, unblemished, the human warmth and generosity of his people. Perhaps, in spite of new and old colonialisms, in his veins, under his velvety skin and stylish clothes, Africa — the ancestors' soul-land — still throbs irrepressibly.

They part with a handshake. Their future partner—it looks as if it's now a done deal—helps Zoe to mount Jolly before taking the path back to Mont Rochelle. As they trot away, Zoe turns and watches him walking straight ahead with elegant ease, as if he were crossing Fifth Avenue instead of an alfalfa field at the tipping end of Africa, carrying a patent leather briefcase instead of a plastic cooler bag.

André quickens his horse's pace and she does the same.

— 9 —
AUNT ADÈLE

Peeling potatoes, shelling beans, slicing onions: Sometimes simple manual tasks help one to slip out of one's thoughts. Zoe busies herself on the chopping board under Georgina's supervision. She has decided to spend her last afternoon at the Cape with her, in the kitchen. But this doesn't help to keep her mind at bay. Thoughts come rushing to her, wave after wave. *I can't resume my daily routine at the lab as if nothing had happened. I won't stand my colleagues' pitiful looks. I won't bear the sudden emptiness of my house in the city. My project is too far-fetched. I will never be able to convince Kuyper to send me into the nowhere.*

"Are you done with those aubergines?" Georgina urges her into action. After Zoe told her about Dario's accident, her *aia* is even more considerate of her needs. Precious Georgina, always so present, yet always so discreet—like tens of thousands of other mixed-blood maidservants, all shrouded in invisibility within white households, their lives thwarted by the master's needs. How many *aias* have remained silent, buried their secrets, let tears fall between the folds of daily laundry, onto polished Sunday mass shoes, over weekly bread dough? How many sorrows have been swallowed by silence, undetected?

Zoe's memory races back to her childhood.

She isn't thirteen yet and still wears braids. On this spring day, while at school, she feels a warm fluid trickle down the inside of her thighs—she is bleeding and her apron is already stained. Too ashamed to let anyone notice, she waits for recess to sneak out of the class and run home with a kerchief between her legs. It takes her less than an hour to reach the Finistère.

She is about to enter the kitchen—her fingers already on the door handle—when she hears someone grunting, perhaps moaning, then her aia *sobbing, begging in a low voice:* "Nee baas, baas nee." *Startled, she flings the door open. Georgina's plump body is mercilessly thrown over the kneading board—her breasts, uncovered, sinking into the bread dough; her skirt up to her waist. A man is holding her head pressed against the board, while harshly thrusting his hips against her buttocks. That man is Willem. His furious gaze for being caught in such a brutal act freezes her. But what stuns Zoe even more is Georgina's shameful look, her eyes encrusted with tears and flour, her mouth stiffened in a desperate grimace.*

Zoe stands there for a brief eternity, horrified, before rushing out and hiding among the grapes, in the furthest field from the house. She remains there, protected by a sea of green leaves, blood dripping copiously down her legs, until Georgina finds her. Less than six months have passed since her parents' death and Zoe has just become a woman.

"Please, my baby, don't tell anyone," Georgina pleads as she dries Zoe's tears with her apron. "If your aunt finds out she will send me away."

"He is the one who must leave, not you!"

"It's not that simple, my precious. The baas *is never wrong. And she needs him to run the farm. She would never manage by herself. While me, there are plenty of maids like me."*

"Nee, *you're my* aia, *my only one!"*

Georgina is thirty-two and has four children to support. Zoe knows that. On that day, though, her aia *tells her something else. Two years ago her husband left to work in the mines in Jo'burg. After he stopped sending money, she went to look for him and found him drunk in a* shebeen *in Soweto. He had lost his job, but wouldn't go back home with her. His excuse was that he was too ashamed to look into his children's eyes. She spat at him and left. Georgina's story is short and bleak, but effective. Willem will stay then, unpunished. He is a monster and the world is cruel. In tears, Zoe promises to keep her mouth shut. Her* aia *hugs her tightly, rocking back and forth, rocking in their pain.*

Since then, they have never talked about that day. That day, Zoe discovered how bitterly she could hate someone. She promised to herself she would never forgive Willem for what he did, for what he could still do.

Back in her bedchamber, Zoe takes Aunt Charlotte's diary out and opens it at the page where she has placed her tassel. She takes a slow, deep breath and starts reading.

Franschhoek, January 16, 1897

Poor Aunt Adèle, she must be seriously worried about what might happen to me; otherwise, she would have never told me her story. "Charlotte," she started, "I know I have sinned. Do not judge me for that." Her pain was so obvious that I had to hug her. She looked so tiny and helpless under that starched bonnet of hers. She recovered quickly, though, and gestured to let her speak. As I did in my previous entry, I'll try to relate her story as faithfully as possible, with the only help of my memory.

She couldn't sleep, she said. Aunt Desirée had died and her story about Gustave's curse haunted her. She would lie awake, eyes wide open, contemplating her barren future. In the end, she convinced herself that she had to ask the help of a sangoma, *a shaman. She thus started making inquiries among their home servants, their labourers and those of other farms. She did it in the most discreet way so as not to arouse any suspicion. It took her almost a year to find out that the most powerful diviner-healer of the region was named Unathi and lived fifty kilometres away from their farm—a whole day's horse ride.*

She now had to find a way to leave the farm unnoticed. If she tried to secretly slip away, her father would order his Khoikhoi hunters to follow her tracks and bring her back. Neither could she ask openly for his permission; if she confessed the truth, sooner or later everyone—starting from their predikant, *her father's closest friend—would find out about the curse and no one would want to have anything to do with the influential family of the Du Plessis. Thus, she kept quiet and waited for the spring* Nagmaal, *when all the families in the valley would load their wagons and head for Stellenbosch; there, they would spend four days together, celebrating holy communion, eating, dancing, socializing.*

"On the morning they left, I pretended I didn't feel well," aunt told me. She feigned a fever and promised father she would join them on horseback as soon as she recovered; Xabbo, their most trusted servant, would escort her. Instead, one hour later she was riding north-east. Xabbo was with her and increasingly concerned about her baas' *daughter's flight off the farm — if they found out, he would be punished harshly for not having stopped her.*

They rode all day. When they reached Unathi's village, it was already getting dark and Aunt Adèle was exhausted. "As we entered the village, any hint of bravery I was left with quickly slipped away," she said. But it was too late to go back.

The chief received her in his hut and she offered him the tobacco and cornmeal she and Xabbo had brought with them. In the basic Xhosa learned since childhood from the house servants, she told him she wanted to see the medicine man.

"I tried not to show it, but I was terrified," she said. I bet she did: a white woman, alone, accompanied by a Khoikhoi, in the midst of a Xhosa kraal!

The chief invited Aunt Adèle to share a meal in his tent with his wives. When, later, the women led her to Unathi's hut, she literally had to drag herself, as much as she was overtaken by fatigue. She found herself sitting in front of an old man, barely dressed, his hips wrapped in a leopard skin. In the dim light of a small fire, she could scarcely make out his wrinkled face, his chest adorned with necklaces made from cowrie shells, his braided hair and beaded-headdress topped with porcupine quills.

Aunt started explaining why she was there, but the medicine man raised his hand and invited her to be quiet. He took a satchel made of steenbok skin and threw the contents on the mat between them. A collection of bones, stones, shells and small, smoothed objects tumbled out, creating a pattern. The sangoma *looked intently at it, then frowned. Three times he threw his bones and three times the rhino's horn fell with its tip pointing at aunt. Only then Unathi spoke, saying that the white woman had a powerful enemy, an unclean spirit. He didn't know if his medicine was as powerful. He then sent her to sleep and told her to come back in the early morning.*

Aunt left the sangoma's *hut and reached Xabbo, who by then had made a fire for them and prepared their bedding. She sank into a deep, dreamless sleep and woke up with the first light. Unathi was already waiting for her at the entrance of his hut. A pot was simmering on the fire; the* sangoma *poured its dark, steaming content into a bowl, which he then handed to her. At that point, Aunt Adèle was terrorized. She still remembers Unathi's words: "You must be ready to fight the evil spirit. Alone. I can only help you to see your enemy."*

It was a bitter, disgusting concoction, with bits of shredded bark floating on the surface. As soon as she was finished, she started gagging, but the sangoma *told her she would need to hold on till she was among her own again. Xabbo had already saddled their horses and off they went.*

It was a hellish journey. She kept shivering, felt fever rising. And the nausea: The more she tried to dismiss it, the more it grew. She was increasingly weak and struggled to stay in the saddle; Xabbo rode by her side, supporting her when she felt faint. She covered the last stretch of the trail in a semi-conscious state, leaning on the mare's neck. When they finally reached the farm, at twilight, Xabbo dragged her to her bed and stood by her side all night, while the fever went up and she started to rave.

"This, at least, is what he told me the next day," aunt said. "In truth, I remember very little of that night." What she remembers well, though, is the scream. It came from within, like a black beast, and invaded her throat. That's when she began to throw up furiously. "I was sure I would die in my vomit," she told me. Instead, at dawn, it was all over and aunt made Xabbo swear never to tell her father, nor any other person, where they had been and what she had done.

Two days later, her father came back to the farm with the whole family and the bulk of the workers; he did not notice anything strange. "At that point, I was sure I had got rid of the curse," aunt said.

Again, I couldn't truly believe my aunt had gone through all this just because of some magical, non-existent black spell. I had kept quiet all the way through her story, but now I could no longer hold my tongue. Aunt Adèle must have read my mind, because she frantically raised her hand to cover my mouth, as if I might swear. She gave me the most sorrowful look as she said: "I'm not done yet."

She went on, with an urgency I had never seen in her before.

She started by explaining that back in those days in Franschhoek men of marriageable age were rare. The few who courted her hadn't piqued her interest. Probably because she had always been secretly in love with François du Preez, their neighbouring farmer's eldest son, a handsome blonde and wild man, ten years senior to her, who had married at the behest of his father the daughter of a wealthy merchant. François often came to their house, to learn from her grandfather the secrets of viticulture and to help in the vineyard when he was needed. Most of the time he ended up staying for dinner. Everyone knew that his wife, a gaunt edgy woman, didn't make him happy.

Twelve months had passed since Aunt Adèle's visit to the witch doctor and, this time, she too attended Nagmaal *in Stellenbosch." After the communal prayers and the supper under the stars, dances followed. On the second evening into the* Nagmaal, *François invited her to dance. "And not just to dance," aunt confessed. "I had spent sleepless nights desiring him. It just felt so right and natural to follow him into the tall grass, under the moonlight." I was shocked by aunt's frankness. I must have showed it on my face, since she hurried to say that she shouldn't talk like that, especially with me, but that I needed to be aware of the consequences of certain decisions.*

I saw Aunt Adèle sigh as she adjusted her bonnet. She had the dreamy gaze of someone lost in blissful memories. "It was an unforgettable night," she said, "My first night of love. And alas! My last one." The following day, she then told me, François was found dead, stabbed in the throat by his drunk father-in-law, who claimed to have seen the two of them walk out of the fields together, hand in hand.

That's how Aunt Adèle ended her story. Since then, she always hopes that any firstborn in our family is a boy. According to her, we females are barren and harmful branches of a cursed lineage.

When I left her, she was still quietly sobbing in her bedchamber. She looked inconsolable.

As she shuts Charlotte's diary, Zoe is left with a lingering perplexity. Despite what has just happened to her, her scientist's mind is still struggling to believe that a curse could haunt a family for generations on end. Rather, she is prone to assume that a series of fatal, tragic coincidences made the Du Plessis women particularly sensitive and superstitious. However, she can't help feeling that her rational mind is slowly slipping away.

— 10 —

THE DECISION

"I CANNOT LET you go, Zoe. I need you here, in the lab."

Right after landing in Johannesburg she headed for Wits' Paleontological Research Unit to meet with Kuyper. A renowned paleoanthropologist, Kuyper rarely misses a chance to let his interlocutor know the prominent facts of his career. In his youth he was assistant to Raymond Dart, the father of South African paleoanthropology and discoverer of the first *Australopithecus* skull. Kuyper also brags about being at Olduvai Gorge in Tanzania with Louis and Mary Leakey when the legendary couple uncovered the fossilized remains of a creature deemed to be one of the earliest members of the genus *Homo*. No doubt an extraordinary figure as a scholar, Kuyper is also the most single-minded person Zoe has ever met. She has just asked him to be sent into the field and his blunt refusal doesn't come as a surprise.

Nonetheless, unexpectedly, he asks: "Where is that you'd want to go, by the way?"

"To northern Namibia, with your permission. To the digs in the Nyae Nyae Conservancy."

"Just around the corner," he says, grumbling.

"I thought I might carry on Dr. Oldani's work up there,"

Zoe says, looking at the map of Africa behind Kuyper's desk. "He believed in his project, in his idea of the Kalahari as the real cradle of early humans."

"Yes, yes," Kuyper says. "I remember what Dario used to say: 'We've just to look for them.' Till today, though, all we got from that hell of a place is a raft of baboon bones."

"These things take time ..." Zoe says.

"Yours is not a rational choice and you know that, Zoe. Presently, there are more promising excavation sites in South Africa if you *truly* wanted to go into the field."

She knows that. But she has made up her mind. No other place will do: She has to go *there*. To do what precisely? Would she be looking for fossils or for Dario's traces instead, tracking his presence in rocks and salt pans and white-hot horizons? Would she try and bring to light the secrets of humanity at its outset or bury her present under a shroud of hot sand? Either way, she must leave.

Kuyper rises and starts pacing around the office, his hands sternly behind his back.

"A woman, alone, in the desert," he says, glaring at Zoe lounging seemingly relaxed in the upholstered armchair in front of his desk. "Not to mention that I would be left without my best researcher here at the lab."

Zoe half-smiles. She is well acquainted with Kuyper's way of dissuading his collaborators from engaging in projects that are not in line with his priorities by flattering them. This time, though, she won't be taken in. She won't budge. She is ready to forgo everything, even her work in the Department.

Meanwhile, Kuyper has resumed his seat.

"What about the upcoming conference in London?" he

asks, tapping his fingers. "Weren't you supposed to present your findings on Lady J there?"

Another tactic of his: Lady J is Zoe's most important project, two years of hard work. It will bring notoriety, no doubt.

"I could ask Piet to do it. He's been helping a lot with the project. He'd love the opportunity," she says feigning carelessness.

Kuyper frowns, rubbing his cheek. Then he starts to nervously shuffle the papers on his desk, as if he could find in there the answer to her request.

There is a long silence.

Zoe glances at the glass skull on the director's desk. He uses it as a paperweight.

"Dario was a brilliant scientist," Kuyper finally says, his voice shifting to a softer tone. "He'd have gone a long way. It's a big loss for all of us."

It doesn't bode well. The sympathetic note means he's about to deny her request. Zoe lowers her head to look down at her runners, as if they could oblige her sudden need to be out of that room, that building, that city, that country.

"You're right," Kuyper says. "The excavation in Namibia made as much sense before, when Dario advocated for it, as it does now, despite the latest setback."

Zoe raises her head and, for the first time since she has entered his room, purposefully looks him in the eye.

"You're an accomplished researcher, Zoe, although a tad young." Kuyper twitches a half-smile. "I'd better send you up there, work up a sweat."

The glass skull now reflects the director's fingers, steepled on the desk.

"Besides, it wouldn't be productive to keep you here," he says, shaking his head. "You know me, Zoe, I can't stand people who work unwillingly. Let's thus try to mix business with the inevitable."

She keeps quiet, as if afraid he might change his mind.

"There are only two conditions," Kuyper says, again shuffling the papers on his desk.

She leans forward.

"Firstly, you'll have to send me reports. They can be short, but at least bi-weekly updates."

No problem there.

"Secondly, the funds already allocated for Dario's expedition can barely cover another eighteen months of fieldwork. I need some results within the year. Otherwise, I'll have to call it off."

He's giving her a chance. For real.

"*Dankie*," she says quietly. The lump in her throat doesn't allow more than that.

"Let's hope you don't mess up things up there as much as you did with your hair."

The interview is over. Zoe stands up and stretches her hand across the desk. Kuyper squeezes it firmly.

"I suppose you want to leave as soon as possible?"

"In a week, if I manage."

"Then go ahead, you don't have much time to crank it up. But don't forget: The budget is tight."

She nods and moves quickly to the door. Her hand is already on the handle.

"Do you remember Koma, the shaman at Schmidtsdrift?"

"*Ja, waarom*?"

"I was thinking of taking him with me. He knows those places, he grew up there."

"It's up to you, Zoe, I'm giving you carte blanche. But bring me something worth the effort."

"I will."

Is it a promise to Kuyper? To herself? To Dario's memory? Even she can't tell.

❁❁❁

She is out in the sun again, driving through this city of gold and misery. Here, even the manicured gardens, watered each day by armies of Blacks in rubber boots, are fragile only in appearance. Beneath that veil of touching innocence, hostility lurks. This is the wasteland of sharp aloe plants, razor grass and trees whose trunks are studded with thorns.

She won't go to the morgue. She won't bind Dario's last memory to the penetrating smell of formaldehyde and the cold light of fluorescent fixtures. She won't go back to the autopsy rooms where in her university years she dissected corpses—real flesh and bones—of young black boys killed in the cross-fire of anti-apartheid demonstrations. Instead, upon leaving the university campus she drives into the CBD and parks the car close to the corner of Rissik and Market Street. Standing there, Zoe inspects the sidewalk where Dario died as if she could still find traces of him, or make one last contact. She is oblivious to the car horns, the cries of street vendors, the beggars' litanies droning around her like distant background noise.

After a while she starts walking and, without realizing

it, reaches Diagonal Street. She sees again Dr. Naidoo's *muti* shop, where Blacks and a growing number of Whites go to be treated with herbs and potions. The showcase is packed with baboon skulls, lizard legs and ampoules of lion fat. She observes how this side of the road is being reflected in the glass panels of the skyscraper that De Beers built like the facets of a diamond not less than fifteen years ago, when the city was still *the city*.

On one side of the street stand financial markets and men in pin-striped suits; on the other, sorcerers and *sangomas.* Right here, in the open heart of downtown Johannesburg, Africa and the West stare blankly at each other—the symbols of Anglo-Saxon economic power neatly juxtaposed against a parallel realm of African subconscious.

This is what you were looking for when you passed through here, Dario: a place where the remote past, present and future seem to operate in the same time frame. At least you chose where *to die.*

— 11 —

RASTA SAM

THE NEWS OF Zoe's imminent departure has created a stir at the department. She is aware of the general discontent about her appointment—especially among those who had hoped to replace Dario in the Kalahari. She plans to be in the field for six months straight, with two-to-three-week breaks in between.

"It's an eternity, up there," Piet told her.

Almost every male colleague feels compelled to provide his bit of advice on the logistics of fieldwork in remote areas; and yet—as she has soon discovered—behind her back most of them are staking money against her capacity for endurance. One morning, as she nears the coffee-room, she overhears a flurry of comments.

"Two months and she'll be back to contemplate her fate in Kuyper's glass skull."

"Too young for the desert."

"Too inexperienced."

"Too spoiled."

There is some truth in their comments. She has indeed experienced life in tented camps located kilometres away from the nearest village, both in Tanzania and Botswana, and worked in several excavation sites in South Africa, but she has never been in charge of an expedition. She feels awkward, not up to the task. As a result, she keeps doggedly consulting the Department Fieldwork Manual.

"Are you done with your preparations?" Robert Stanford asks her as she walks into the room. Robert is a veteran of field research, a vigorous man in his fifties with a sunburned face. He wears a faded flannel shirt, khaki trousers and dusty boots, as if he'd just come out of the bush. That's part of his legend, isn't it? Don't be envious, she tells herself.

"Not really. Still looking for a driver. Anyone in mind?" she replies sucking up her pride.

Robert furrows his thick brows, taking a sip at his coffee. His eyes suddenly light up.

"Here you go, Sam Kaleni! Should've thought of him straight away," he cries as he takes his pipe out of the shirt pocket and starts scratching its insides with the tip of a pocket knife.

"A brilliant mechanic," he adds after a pause, almost muttering to himself. "A great travel companion too."

"Can he also work as a digger?"

"I guess so, although I can't vouch for that bit," he says, giggling in a self-amused tone. "I'll call him up. Let's see how he feels about going back to Bushmanland."

"Was he there, already?"

"Oh, he'll tell you himself," he replies, putting the pipe in his mouth without lighting it. "If he deems so."

Zoe notices her colleague's reluctance to provide more information on the man.

"A Zulu, I guess from his surname."

"You bet."

"*Goed*," Zoe replies. Then she pauses, abashed by her

spontaneous reaction. She is meant to travel over three thousand kilometres with a black man she doesn't know. Why, then, should this detail about his ethnicity reassure her? Why should she prefer certain Blacks over others? Dario was quick to detect this ethnic bias among her people: He called it the "Boers' Zulu mystique." He also attempted an explanation: "It seems the fierce battles your people and the Zulus fought against each other paved the way to a form of mutual respect and consideration."

He was right. In the days of apartheid, the Boers exploited tribal favouritism to grant the Zulus a slightly better status than that of other black tribes. On their part, the Zulus reciprocated by showing a slightly less antagonistic attitude towards the Afrikaners. Apartheid may now be gone, but the ethnic mystique hasn't faded yet, and Zoe has just realized how much she, too, is under its spell.

"Are you with us?" her colleague asks, noticing she seems no longer listening to him.

"I'm sorry, just lost in thought. Thanks for this, Robert."

"You owe me one," he says as he makes for the exit raising the pipe over his head in a gesture of salutation.

Dario's camp up north in the Kalahari is currently manned by five workers. Their foreman has been informed of Dr. Oldani's death and is now waiting for a replacement. Zoe doubts the workers expect to have a woman as their new boss. To be on the safe side and avoid disrupting an established pattern, she is going to stick to Dario's way of running the camp.

She has arranged for a bush plane to land every three months in Tsumkwe, bring fresh supplies and fly her crew in and out. Tsumkwe is the closest village to the base camp and is only an hour flight to Windhoek international airport, which connects to all major South African cities with regular flights. If she wished, she could fly. Instead, she'll drive back to the camp the Land Rover Dario brought to Johannesburg, on what would be his last trip. Showing up at the camp with that car and a bunch of fresh supplies —she hopes—might boost her chances to be made welcome by the workers. In any case, she needs to bring a new *bakkie* up there, thus sharing the long ride with the pick-up driver makes sense.

Early in the morning, Zoe called her friend Shaida, a social worker at Schmidtsdrift, and asked her to see whether Koma and his wife Namkwa would be willing to return to the Kalahari with her. The base camp has been set up in the northeast corner of Namibia, not far from one of the few remaining !Kung settlements. For the two of them it would mean going home after years of exile. Now, Shaida has called her back in a flurry of excitement: "You should've seen them, Zoe. They've even improvised a little dance in my office to thank you for this unexpected offer."

Her friend agrees to put the old couple on a train to Vryburg; Zoe will pick them up there, on her way to the North. That same evening, Robert calls her to confirm Sam is free and can be part of the expedition. She now feels relieved: All the pieces seem to be falling into place.

The morning after, however, when she meets the new driver, she silently curses her colleague.

A man in his late thirties with long braided hair tucked into a large colourful wool knit beanie stands grinning in front of her. A deep scar runs vertically through his left jaw; his bloodshot, dreamy eyes reveal he's not insensitive to the lure of *dagga*. *Bugger, he sent me a Rasta!*

"*Howzit, Professor Du Plessis*?" Sam Kaleni greets her in a jovial voice. He slips his hand around her thumb, following the traditional handshake among black people. She awkwardly goes into the moves, obligingly. Many Whites are now using this way of greeting to show their liberal views and their—often improbable—acquaintance with black culture. She finds it patronizing.

The young man is well built, though slim, and displays a broad grin that somewhat reminds her of her brother. She restrains from smiling back at him, feeling she must put the record straight from the start.

"Robert told me you're an excellent driver and mechanic. However, I'm heading to an excavation camp, and I need a digger as well as a driver."

"*Mies*, you're buying here two men for the price of one," Sam replies, switching from English to Afrikaans and placing his right hand on his heart. There is something irreverent, tainted with self-amusement, in his eyes and body language. Zoe's black-skinned countrymen are gradually losing all trace of subjection to the white *baas*. She still has to fully get used to it. Since she was a little girl, the subliminal consciousness of white entitlement has seeped through her skin. Every now and then it resurfaces, uncensored. It happened only a few months ago, she now remembers, on the day when a shop assistant in Johannesburg addressed her in a rude manner. *Only a few years ago you'd have never dared speak to me in that tone*, she heard her saying to herself. She was horrified: Those were the words of a diehard Boer seething with anger, not of a presumably soft-spoken, enlightened cosmopolitan.

The imminent departure makes her restless. Her adventure spirit is suddenly gnawing at her. Did she ever seriously contemplate the idea of pursuing a career working as a lab rat, fully bent on achieving professional celebrity? *No way.* She has always known she belongs to the other kind of scientists: those who love to gain their honours in the field, digging their path at the margins, bearing the Spartan hardships of the frontier—far from the clamour and worldly comforts. She may well remain an obscure researcher for the rest of her life, but she will be out there, in the scrub, under the big sky of Africa. Most of all, away from *eGoli*, this "city of gold" built out of hundreds of mine landfills encroaching on its inhabitants like malignant growths.

On the afternoon before their departure Zoe goes to check one last time the Land Rover and the *bakkie*, both crammed to capacity. As she enters the garage she catches the unmistakably sweet smell of the *dagga*. Sam pushes himself out from under the 4x4, a wrench in his right hand, and with elegant insouciance offers her his *zol.* Zoe shakes her head, turning down her mouth with a look of disapproval.

"Any problems?" she asks, looking at him askance.

"Not at all."

"*Goed*, I'll see you tomorrow morning, then. Half past four, ready to go."

Teasing her, Sam replicates the subdued tone of black servants: "*Yebo, Mejuffrou.*"

All this would perhaps amuse her, if she were in an altogether different situation, in another stage of her life, in another country. But here and now, she cannot take any pleasure in jokes, or levity.

Sam grounds the butt of his *zol* under the sole of his work boot before raising his head and meeting her eye.

"You can't wait to leave, isn't it, Miss?" he asks, switching again back to English. And then adds, his head slightly bent on one side, his dreadlocks dangling from underneath his hat: "Who could blame you?"

"Bugger," she says again under her breath, addressing colleague Robert Stanford as she turns and walks briskly out of the garage.

— 12 —

ON THE ROAD

"It's one of those places where the ghosts of apartheid still hover menacingly," Dario wrote in his notebook. Zoe has been reluctant to stop over in Vryburg, asking Koma and his wife to get there by train. But the R31 that will take them to Rietfontein and from there across the border into Namibia cuts through the heart of former Transvaal. Hastily and prosaically renamed North-West Province, the cradle of Afrikanerdom retains its irreconcilable cultural identity.

Not much seems to have changed in this part of the country since the high days of racial segregation. The Rainbow Nation's concept of equal citizenship among South Africa's eleven tribes is no more than a thin veneer over the true colours of this Boer stronghold. What Dario wrote no longer than a year ago is as valid as ever: In rural South Africa as everywhere else, race remains central in establishing what people think of each other and, consequently, in determining how they behave toward one another.

The previous night, before falling asleep, she re-read that passage in Dario's diary in which he dissects her country giving it little hope: "Two conflicting perceptions of reality are at stake here. Blacks are embittered; to them things are not changing fast enough after the promises of the New South Africa. They are growing impatient and many are increasingly unwilling to keep on playing 'Mr. Nice.' Whites, for their part, believe they have already paid their dues by accepting a Black majority government. What's more, they resent the stigma still hanging over them and the growing lack of prospect for the future. In their eyes, the *swart gevaar* is no longer a threat but has become a reality. As a consequence, many prefer to leave for less troubled frontier countries—Canada and Australia being top of their list."

But not the hard-liners who live here, Zoe thinks as she drives into Vryburg, or in Schweizer-Reneke, Louis Trichardt, Ventersdorp. *These backveld Boers won't budge. They are here to stay. On their own terms.*

The train on which Koma and his wife are travelling is late. The streets are deserted and, despite the early hour, blindingly white with sheets of heat. Sam and Zoe make their way to a nearby pub. Inside, the place is cool, dark and almost empty. The bartender turns slowly to check out the new customers. He is a blocky white man in his fifties with a bull neck bulging out of a military green shirt and a truculent demeanour. As he sees Sam, he furrows his thick eyebrows and assumes a grim, unfriendly expression. The only other customers, three farmers sitting at a corner table, stop digging into their breakfast to watch the odd couple that has just entered in their line of sight. The place falls into an eerie silence.

Zoe hesitates, standing by the entrance door. She would gladly turn tail and go back into the shimmering heat. Sam walks past her and heads resolutely for the lavatory.

She moves toward the counter and as she rummages in

her satchel asks softly, trying to keep a low key: "Two sodas, please."

The bartender takes the two drinks from the fridge and hands them to her with a wry smile.

"*Twee koeledranke*," he says in Afrikaans while gazing up at her, marking his cultural space like a predator would scent mark his territory.

"*Dankie*," Zoe says, looking away.

Sam is back by her side now, scouring the place, his teeth bared sardonically.

❁❁❁

She hastens to finish her soda water, pays her dues and motions him to head for the exit. Instead, her companion takes a 10-rand note from his pocket and places it on the counter with studied casualness.

"Marlboro, *asseblief*," he says, looking into the bartender's eyes. There are four decades of segregation behind Sam's defiant and eloquent look, she can't help thinking. Yes man, it implies, even in Vryburg a black can now sit in a pub next to a white woman, speak English and be served by a racist. With equally theatrical slowness, never lowering his eyes, the bartender puts the pack of cigarettes on the counter together with the change. His gaze, too, full of disdainful condescension, says it all: You can sit here and show off your white girlfriend, but to me you remain a *kaffir*.

How on earth are we going to mend all this? Zoe asks herself while rushing for the exit in desperate need for fresh air.

❁❁❁

The train has entered the station and is about to leave again. As she and Sam cross the street, Zoe spots them: a little man and a little woman standing on the sunny sidewalk, waiting near their bundles. They look so out of place, almost lost, in this asphalt world; they, of all people, who can read the great book of deserts and orient themselves in the nothingness of burning sands. Even here, though, they maintain their unmistakable bearing—relaxed, yet alert—always present within themselves and to the world around them.

The moment Namkwa sees Zoe, she starts clapping her hands with joy. Her eyes are hardly visible through the thick pattern of wrinkles in her face. She wears a sun-faded scarf knotted behind her head and a patched flowered dress with white lace around the edges. With her apricot-brown skin and heavy-lidded eyes, she looks like a native American goddess wrapped in a doll dress. She squeezes Zoe's hands and smiles, revealing a handful of missing teeth. Koma instead, his face straight and enigmatic, just holds his eyes firmly on hers. Those eyes speak of trust and dignity. They also silently convey a resolution: There will be no going back to Schmidtsdrift.

Zoe turns towards Sam, who has kept himself discreetly in the background, and introduces him. To her surprise, he greets the couple in the crackling, snappy language, full of click sounds, of the !Kung people. The couple's creased faces brighten even more and an animated conversation ensues, of which Zoe doesn't catch a word.

"How come you know their language?" she asks him at the first opportunity.

"I lived among the Ju/'hoansi for over two years," he replies with studied casualness as he adjusts his beanie.

"Wow!" Zoe is truly impressed: Ju/'hoansi is no ordinary word; it's mostly used by the !Kung of Nyae Nyae when referring to themselves. Sam has even pronounced it with the right click in the right place — Dju-kwa-si — recreating the sound of a cork popping out. Her mechanic-cum-digger is far more acquainted with the base camp area than she assumed.

"Why didn't you tell me?"

"I thought Professor Stanford already did, *Mejuffrou*."

"It's typical of Robert to omit the relevant facts," she mutters glancing at her watch. The stopover in Vryburg has lasted all too long.

"*Nou goed*, let's get moving."

Once again Zoe checks the oil and fuel gauges, as well as the radio contact between the two vehicles. The Land Rover responds smoothly to her driving. Koma is sitting beside her, Namkwa in the back. From time to time Zoe looks at the old woman through the rear-view mirror. She sits still and composed, her arms lying at her sides, watching the modern world roll by in front of her at eighty kilometres per hour — she, who has walked slowly her entire life.

For the first hundred kilometres, no one speaks; they are all overwhelmed, although for different reasons.

Zoe has her eyes fixed on the road, while her thoughts

run wild. The doubts that have troubled her during the preparations and that she has stubbornly pushed back now return with greater insistence. She has let herself be lured by a scorching desert, a distant world of heat and dust. The thought that she should have been less impulsive now creeps in. She isn't even sure what counts more: the wish to chase her lover's dreams or the attempt to run away from hers.

So many times in these last days has she pored over Dario's journal, trailing her finger over his twisted, almost illegible handwriting. Luckily, he jotted down most of his notes in English, perhaps to allow other colleagues to read them; only occasionally did he add a few words in Italian, probably not knowing their English translation; even more rarely did he write whole sentences in his mother tongue. Was it because his thoughts were too intimate and personal? She will need to have them translated. With her right hand she feels Dario's small notebook in her breast pocket. For the first time since his death, she feels him close.

Just as well. Let's vanish into the bush, you and me.

Zoe turns briefly towards Koma. The old man points his index finger towards something high above, beyond the windshield: A blue immensity is opening up in front of them. Soon they will be under his sky.

— 13 —
KALAHARI

"THIS DESERT is unnerving. It doesn't have any of the mystique or the charm of the Sahara," Dario had written of the Kalahari in his field journal. "It's just a vast, desolate expanse of yellow earth, scattered with sharp-blade grasses, thorny shrubs and acacias. Only its southern section, which ventures into South African territory, has spectacular red sand dunes, with solitary black-maned lions roaming the open pans. Occasionally, mighty baobabs rise amidst the arid plains. It takes twenty to thirty metres of duct tape to wrap their trunk just once. Some of those giants are more than a thousand years old."

The baobabs. Zoe thinks of them as "the lords of time," watching unperturbed the passing of the decades, growing imperceptibly, further strengthening their compact bark, as smooth and hard as stone. Bushmen revere them and would never camp in their vicinity. They believe they have holy water in their trunk and are full of *n/om*, the energy source that gives life to the universe and all its creatures.

The sun mercilessly beats down on their vehicles as they drive through the flat plains. Only a few stops to stretch their legs, drink coffee from the thermos and have a quick bite from their *padkos* interrupt the whole-day journey. They are all eager to get to their destination—their destiny, perhaps. She runs a hand over her forehead beaded with sweat, then glances sideways at her companions. They have asked her to keep the air conditioning off and the temperature in the cabin has become unbearably stifling. They sit wooden-still and placid like two *kokerbooms*: yes, like those centennial desert markers with branches thrust upside down praying silently towards a merciless sky.

When they reach the border between South Africa and Namibia the sun has already started crouching in the western sky, opening a red wound in its blueness. There is no fence, just a signboard that indicates the end of a country and the beginning of another. In front of them, more of the same solitary gravel road seems to disappear into an absolute stillness. Hundreds of kilometres of nothingness stretch around them in all directions. A solitary camelthorn tree is the only hint of green. Two bored South African border guards sitting on plastic chairs in front of a small cabin stop their game of cards as Zoe pulls over and rolls out of the car. The two soldiers look perplexed at the odd travelling party—a red-haired woman, a Rasta and two old Bushmen.

"Where are you headed?" the bulkier and blonder of the two asks.

"Up north, to Tsumkwe," Zoe answers.

"Doing what exactly?" His blue eyes now on hers.

"I'm with Wits University. We'll be looking for fossils."

"Then, no need to go further, *Mies*!" the border guard cries breaking into a grin. "Here we are, two forgotten skeletons in the middle of nowhere."

Zoe smiles feebly, but doesn't reply. They all follow the man in uniform into the cabin and wait for him to check and stamp their documents. When he is done he gestures them towards a door in the middle of the cabin. They walk through it and into Namibia to meet another couple of bored guards. To pass the time, one of them—a skinny black man with greying hair—is crotcheting lace.

"Not much traffic, eh?" Sam says as he hands over his passport.

Neither guard replies. Instead, both take their time examining Koma's and Namkwa's papers.

"First time I see a bushman's passport," the skinny one says.

Ja, Zoe thinks, they too now have to go through borders. They knew only freedom and unrestrained movement. Now they need to prove they have a surname, an identity, even a domicile. Their births must be registered, their marriages sanctioned. Like everyone else, they have to conform to *this* modernity. Traditional practices and rituals are leftovers for money-making folklore, for the tourists' sake. The stamp falls with a thud on the old couple's papers. It sounds like a life sentence—for a whole people.

❁❁❁

They camp fifty kilometres past the border post, in a faintly surreal nowhere land. Only a family of warthogs scuttles about as Koma lights a small fire. Then the scene retreats again into its stream of hushed stillness.

Exhausted, Zoe gulps down her sandwich before

reaching for her sleeping bag. While rummaging through her backpack with the help of a torch she comes upon Aunt Charlotte's diary. Despite the fatigue, she takes it out and sifts through the pages until she finds her ancestor's last note. She steadies the torch on it and reads it again, knowing those words will now take on a new meaning.

Franschhoek, November 15, 1899

Today we buried my lover. I didn't believe my aunties, mistaking their knowledge for mere superstition. I am upset and desperate. Above all, I am angry.

What was wrong—or sinful—or degrading—in offering myself to the only man I wanted?

I still cannot accept the idea that the guilt of one man, albeit tainted with the blood of many innocents, may fall on his descendants in such a blind manner.

I hate these people, my people—their narrow-mindedness, their obtuse religion, their self-serving morality.

There must be a way to break free from it all.

After that, Aunt Charlotte didn't write anything else. What follows are the memories of her young granddaughter Claire—Aunt Claire. Zoe snaps the diary closed, too tired for anything else.

Through the darkness come the click sounds of the conversation between Sam and Koma.

It's their first night under a star-filled Namibian sky, but she takes little notice of it. Her eyelids close heavily, without warning.

❁❁❁

The gravel road is a straight line of dust. On either side of it the rocky plains stretch away indefinitely. There are no trees. Only the spikes of giant aloes challenge from time to time the dullness of flat planes. They have been driving the whole day, the second of their trip, and the sun has moved down once again, stretching the shadows of their vehicles on the ground.

"Baster Country," Sam's voice croaks through the two-way radio.

In the distance, looming over the desolate and arid plain, Zoe makes out the red, black and white flag of the Free Republic of Baster.

"Roger that," she replies.

"Proud bunch," Sam says.

"You bet," she says, knowing what Sam is hinting at. Turning a racist insult into a stern declaration of identity: That's what the offspring of Cape Dutch settlers and Khoikhoi women did. Their odd mix of Hottentot traditions, Afrikaans language and strict Calvinism must have intrigued Dario. After driving across the Basters' hot, arid "promised land," he filled several pages of his journal writing about the thirty thousand of them still living there, a hundred years after their fathers fled the Cape area to escape discrimination from white colonists. "Now they are facing the hostility of the ruling black tribes, who greatly suffered under Pretoria's protectorate," Dario wrote, adding his doleful conclusion: "Once again, they are on the wrong side of history. The mixed loyalty springing from mixed blood won't be easily forgiven."

That night, they camp on the outskirts of Rehoboth,

the Basters' settlement. The day after, early in the morning, they're in Windhoek.

The capital of the newly independent Namibia still bears the imprints of its distant German colonial past. They drive through Bismarck Strasse and Bahnhof Strasse and park near the neo-Gothic construction of Christuskirche. The café where they stop for breakfast offers in its menu *Bratwurst mit Sauerkraut* and *Apfelstrudel*; the waiter addresses Zoe in German. She orders for everyone then walks up to the window overlooking the sidewalk. The scene is almost surreal: A Prussian blue, cloudless sky towers over fanciful early nineteenth-century houses with terracotta roofs and extravagant spires; a black newsboy strolls up and down trying to sell the *Frankfurter Allgemeine*, a local version of the German daily newspaper.

Everything around here looks like a stage for actors who have long left. The Whites are few, the descendants of the early German settlers even fewer. Dario didn't miss the irony of it all. Zoe takes his notebook out of the breast pocket and reads again through his notes: "People are mostly Bantu-speaking Ovambos ... The other local ethnicities were decimated during the colonial administration in what was then German Südwesafrika ... The Herero and the Nama tried a rebellion in 1904 and were crushed to the point of genocide ... more than 100,000 killed ... mass murder for mass land-grab. Despite it all, Windhoek hasn't lost its taste for Sacher Torte."

❁ ❁ ❁

They quickly leave behind the small desert capital with its incongruous traces of white Bavaria and head for

Grootfontein, 450 kilometres to the north-east. There they refuel and fill their reserve tanks. "No petrol ahead," reads the signpost at the beginning of the dirt road that starts in a few metres. From then on, they will be on their own. While she is paying, Zoe catches her reflection in the small mirror behind the counter. She sees a woman with sad eyes, the stumps of her cropped hair hidden under a sun-bleached headscarf, her khaki shirt marked by sweat stains. She can barely recognize herself.

They drive for another four hours through a plain of flat horizons, leaving a long cloud of dust in their wake as they bump along over gravel and sand. They pass a few hills and lots of baobabs, but no people and no cars or trucks.

It's late in the afternoon when they finally reach Tsumkwe, the Bushmanland administrative centre and the last outpost before the emptiness of a frontier desert. There isn't much there, and what there is, is spread out. "The village boasts a general store, a bottle store, a school and a thousand inhabitants, mainly Hereros, Kavangos and Bushmen," Dario wrote in his notes. "The Whites are six in all: two rangers of the National Parks Board, a magistrate with his wife and two full-time missionaries."

They drive along the main street, past the police station and a small clinic. At the intersection, where another thin gravel road crosses theirs, they find the only store. Zoe steps off the Land Rover and asks two young boys who are playing in the dust directions for the rangers' house. The kids run ahead of her car, gesturing her to follow them. As they come around a bend, they have to stop. A Bushman has passed out drunk in the middle of the track. Zoe remembers what Dario wrote about the Ovambos in Tsumkwe: "They make a big profit out of the Bushmen's plight. For ten rand the woman running the *shebeen* fills old whisky bottles with wine; each day, home-made beer is brewed in forty-gallon plastic garbage pails; twenty or so Bushmen pass the bottle around, dancing barefoot in the dirt as they drink."

No ancient wisdom there, just pure hell—this is the dark side of places like Tsumkwe, Zoe keeps thinking as the children lead her to a single-story, ranch style house.

The rangers' house is a modest structure, with a corrugated iron roof and cracked red brickwork, surrounded by a garden clearly in need of more care. Soon the sun will sink out of sight as abruptly as it has risen in the morning. Zoe walks up to the veranda and through the screen door sees a lanky man somewhere in his forties, bare-chested and barefoot, in faded military shorts, coming to greet her.

"Daniel Uys?" she asks as the ranger opens the door with one hand, holding a steaming cup of rooibos tea with the other. He has a thin and haggard face and in his deep-set eyes Zoe catches a sort of feverish light. One of those hermits who live on the margins of the civilized world, she guesses.

"*Ja*, it's me. And you're Zoe, right? *Welkom*, I've been waiting for you guys. How was the trek?"

"A schlep, no doubt," Zoe says.

"I told you you wouldn't make it to the camp in one haul. You'll have to stay here for the night."

"You were right. I'm beat."

"I can tell. Come in. I'll put the kettle on."

❁❁❁

Life in the bush teaches you to get straight to the heart of issues and people, doing away with pleasantries and formalities. Though Zoe has never met Daniel before and has only spoken to him a few times via radio in the weeks before, a handshake is enough to establish a comradely relationship. Yet, there is something else in this reciprocal acknowledgment. Our being both white, she presumes: the primeval instinct to look for your own people.

"My colleague Morgan is away at the moment, you can have his room," the ranger says looking at her and then at Sam and the two bushmen standing by the two vehicles. "Your driver can sleep on the couch." They both know that Koma and Namkwa would rather sleep outside. Even in Tsumkwe the houses that the government has assigned to the San people are used primarily as workshops, stores or food pantries. The Bushmen live in the yard, where they build their simple round huts made of sticks, mud and grass.

That evening Zoe takes a long shower, knowing it will be the last real one before the wilderness. She stands beneath the thin water jet thinking of all the things people take for granted in some privileged pockets of the modern world. A fat slice of humanity has forgotten the sacrifices endured across the ages, when it lived without whirlpools and microwave ovens. She is going back into a world where women are leaving every morning to cut wood and fetch water from a well before they can do their cooking.

❁❁❁

They have a quick dinner outdoors around a garden grill, after which Koma and Namkwa go to look for their people in town. To reciprocate the ranger's hospitality, Zoe has opened a couple of bottles from the crate of Cape Pinot Noir they've brought with them. No reason to wait for some "special occasion," despite what her brother suggested in the accompanying note: The furnace of the Kalahari would spoil the wine in no time. While they enjoy the wine, the conversation turns to Bushmanland. The ranger tells a few anecdotes about his life there and then updates her about the base camp, which he regularly visits during his site inspections of that part of the park.

"Nice chaps you have down there," he says as he cleans the grate with a heavy-duty wire brush. "Dr. Oldani had picked them well, poor bugger!"

Zoe keeps quiet, gazing into the glowing embers. She isn't ready to talk about Dario, nor his death. There's an awkward silence. Sam takes a burning stick from the fire to light his *zol.* After a while, the ranger stands up and goes into the house. He comes back a few minutes later with a big folder under his arm.

"These are drawings I've made of some rock paintings we've recently found in the area," he explains, passing around a bunch of pictures. "Some of them must've been done in the second half of the 19th century, since they show men on horseback, cattle, rifles, covered wagons with teams of oxen. Others might be even twenty to thirty thousand years old."

Zoe looks at the first one. She follows the ochre outline of a human figure painted in white, with an antelope-like head and hooves instead of feet: A therianthrope, most probably a shaman who, in a trance state, took on the power of an animal.

"Beautiful," she says while passing it to Sam.

The ranger rubs his unshaved cheek and then adds: "I can't get enough of them."

Sam blows smoke from his *zol* over the painted scene as if he could revive it by breathing life into it: "Looks like the staging of an after-death experience."

Zoe scans the other pictures: Whoever conceived those drawings was able to convey with a single, virtually uninterrupted line the terror of a zebra on the run, the regal prowess of a lion with prey in its jaws, the elegance of an eland caught silently watching from behind the bushes.

"We still know so little about them," she says. *So much so that we're not even sure what to call them or how they call themselves—First People, Bushmen, San, Khoisan.* Tragically misunderstood, driven off the land they once roamed freely on, enslaved and shot at to the last person before anyone—white or black—took the time to ask them who they were, let alone what they thought about things.

"Just a bunch of crude, rudimentary lines ..." Daniel says, moving his hands while he's talking, reproducing in the air what he has seen in his solitary excursions.

"Yet, so powerful," Zoe finishes the sentence for him. She has caught the hallucinatory glow in the ranger's eyes, as if he had peeked beyond the threshold of reality, in some otherworldly dimension. Looking back at the past few days, she thinks she recognized the same visionary glaze in Sam's eyes too. She shudders. *It's getting harder to discern reality from auto-suggestion, separate delusion from exhaustion.*

"Let's call it a day," she says rubbing her eyes. "We'll leave at dawn, Daniel."

"*Goeienag.* I'll be up to see you off."

❁❁❁

Another clear Namibian dawn is rising from the darkness. They down their coffee standing on the *stoep*, eager to get moving. Daniel feels their impatience and doesn't hold them back.

"I'll come to visit you soon. Every so often I check on Narro's clan," he says mentioning the village leader on whose *Noré* the base camp stands.

"I count on it," Zoe says while climbing on the Land Rover.

The engine starts on the first try.

❁❁❁

They are the last thirty kilometres, and the hardest. The bush, at last, Zoe thinks as her eyes hover over a drabness of shrubs, prickly grass and scrawny camel-thorns. She glances at Namkwa in the rear-view mirror, ever so calm and contained. Now the old woman's eyes are intent on discovering life where she can see only flat desolation. All that she learned in Schmidtsdrift about the Bushmen's way of life comes back in orderly succession. On average, a San woman knows the nutritional and medicinal value of over three hundred plants. Looking at an insignificant stem, she can determine if, half a metre underneath, there is a big tuber swollen with water or a root rich in valuable nutrients. A spiny, low-branching shrub can tell her where to find the larvae of an insect from which to extract the poison for the hunters' arrows. A particular type of grass will help her, if necessary, to abort a pregnant woman.

From mother to daughter, San women have handed down the secrets of the bush. Twenty thousand years of adaptation to a semi-desert eco-system have been preserved across the generations, through the oral histories of the tribe.

❁❁❁

Zoe is busy negotiating a deep pothole in the tiny dirt track when Koma points out something. She follows the direction of his index finger and meets the gentle eyes of a duiker, the tiniest of antelopes; it's staring at them, curious and scared at the same time. Zoe doesn't even have time to bring the car to a stop and switch off the engine—the animal is gone, seeking shelter in the thicket.

"They're so elusive. That's a good sign, isn't it, Koma?"

"*Ja*. The heart is happy to be back."

Zoe searches the arid landscape before starting the engine again. In the sheer stillness, she detects the faintest silver quivering of grass tussocks. And there is this light, unlike any other: clean, sharp, unfiltered. She recalls what Dario wrote in his notebook the first time he entered the Kalahari: "Muscles relax, the mind expands. The vastness enters into the skin like a shot. 'Our' time dissolves."

You and I can only share the poetry of the desert, now.

— 14 —
THE CAMP

FINALLY, AFTER THREE hours spent negotiating the bumpy and sandy dirt track, they reach the camp. It stands in a clearing surrounded by low acacia trees, less than five hundred metres from the Bushmen's *kraal* of Xobaha and fifteen kilometres from the border with Botswana. The military canvas tents have been pitched in a circle.

A burly boy in his mid-twenties walks up to her car, wiping sweat from his face with a kitchen towel.

"*Goeiemôre*," Zoe says in Afrikaans. "You must be Wally."

"*Ja*, Professor Du Plessis, we were waiting for you," he replies with a broad smile. "The others left two hours ago for the pit. I cook and guard the camp."

According to Dario's notes, Wally is a Xhosa. In addition to him and the foreman Moses Mazivila, a Shangaan, the group of diggers includes a Tswana, a Swazi and a Sotho: a small cross-section of multiethnic South Africa, no doubt. She will have to manage her miniature Rainbow Nation with determination, her one card to play as a young woman at the head of her first excavation.

Fifteen minutes later an old, heavily battered *bakkie* stops right outside the camp in a cloud of dust.

"Just in time, Dr. Du Plessis," Moses says, rushing to greet her after Wally called him on the car radio. "We've found three other fragments."

In the last radio contact before Zoe left Johannesburg, the foreman reported the finding of a skull fragment, most probably belonging to an old hominid. *It's a good start. But it's just that, a start.* Every paleoanthropologist's dream is to find a hominid skeleton. Yet, until now, no more than six of them—dating back to various eras and all incomplete—have been found throughout Africa.

"Nice to see you again, Moses," she says shaking the outstretched hand of a tall, ascetically thin middle-aged man. Taking off his cap, he reveals a perfectly bald head, which now shines in the searing light like waxed leather.

"The pleasure is mine, *Mejuffrou*."

When a few years ago Zoe met Moses during an expedition to the Lesotho mountains, she saw for herself the legendary skill of this fossil hunter, the son of a shepherd in the Lowveld with no money and too many children. Moses was only sixteen when he started working as a digger with Phillip Tobias, the other great pioneer of South African paleoanthropology. Tobias was struck by the boy's innate ability to spot the tiniest fossils even where other experts' eyes had already combed the place. In addition to his extraordinary eye for fossils, Zoe's foreman can now boast over thirty years of experience out in the field, in some of the harshest areas of the continent. However, he is not the kind of guy who would brag about it.

"Wally, please help Sam to unload," she cries already heading towards Moses' *bakkie*.

Then, as the foreman starts the engine, she addresses him: "Did you find them in the same spot as the other piece?"

"*Ja*, in the bed of a dried-up river, about five kilometres from here. The dating is still to be confirmed, but we are in the three-million-year-time frame."

In his field journal, Dario mentioned at least four potential sites not far from the base camp, highlighting them on the enclosed map in red pencil. So far, the men have been working on two of these, mainly finding fossil remains of animals: wildebeest jaws, baboon femurs, long giraffe bones.

As he drives with his eyes on the rough and broken ground ahead, Moses opens up, his voice low and croaky: "I'm sorry for what happened to Professor Oldani."

Zoe doesn't turn around to look at him, but lets her eyes roam the expanse of arid scrub savannah. They've left the track now and are following a faint 4x4 trace wandering off across a patch of open woodland. She holds back her tears and says, her voice barely audible above the noise of the engine: "It was a hard blow for all of us."

A long silence follows. Then Moses says: "He had the eye."

❁❁❁

They have entered a river bed. They follow it for a couple of kilometres until they meet a team of men bent under the sun, intent on scouring the ground, palm after palm. They all stand up to greet her, taking their caps off and drying sweat from their faces with dusty kerchiefs.

"These are Shadrack and Lionel, young but capable," Moses says. "And this is Steve. He's been with me for twenty years." Then he turns to point out a couple of spots on the ground. "Here. This is where we found the first fragment and this is where we found the other three."

Zoe feels the desire to touch those holes, push her hands into that soil, but she restrains herself.

"Where are they?" she asks.

Steve takes the fragments out from a small metal box lying at his feet and hands them to her.

Holding the biggest piece between her thumb and index finger, Zoe gathers from its thickness and shape that it could belong to the skull of an *Australopithecus*. You were right, then, she tells herself, acknowledging Dario's ability to identify even in the midst of this featureless desert a potentially favourable site. It's too early to get carried away, nonetheless. On too many occasions the initial discovery of some minute fragments turned out to be an empty promise. In this field more than in any other, scientific celebrity is the product of sheer luck almost as much as of undisputed expertise. What we are looking for are needles of Palaeolithic evidence in the immense haystack of Africa.

At midday, they all return to the base camp in the *bakkie*. Her tent (the same in which Dario slept?) has been pitched with its entrance facing outwards, to offer her some privacy: Zoe feels grateful for this thoughtfulness. She also notices that Namkwa has started to assemble the twig frame of the couple's hut near the camp. In her heart, she hoped the two elders would be living close to her.

"Where are they?" she asks Wally, pointing at the hut.

"At the *kraal*," the cook replies, handing her a cup of tea.

Zoe feels an instinctive bond with the San people and with the Coloured in general. It isn't always the case with the Blacks, she now admits to herself in dismay. She grew up in Africa, but she doesn't know them. There are millions of them in her country, yet — except for her interaction with a bunch of researchers and medical students — she hasn't shared much with them. She doesn't know how they reason, what they really think of Whites, how they judge Whites, or how much they hate Whites.

She cannot forget she was shaken to the bones by the news of that white doctor who had spent his life treating black people at the Baragwanath Hospital in Soweto only to be kicked to death at the height of the township uprisings. The anger stirred by his skin colour obliterated any other emotion or consideration, be it a sense of gratitude, a spark of human compassion or sheer opportunism. The stark reality of events like these, and the awareness of how alien they have seemed to her, is weighing upon her — especially now that she has thrust herself into the African interior. Perhaps the real reason behind the idea of bringing the old San couple with her was the need to have someone closer to her, better known.

❁❁❁

She has her first dinner with the team in the last light of sunset, realizing that none of the workers, except Sam and Moses, would speak to her unless she addresses them first. For them, men from the rural areas of the interior, she remains the white mistress. She will have to find the right way to shape the relations between her and the workers. Now, she is too tired to think about it.

The road trip has been exacting and she goes to sleep

— 15 —

WITH NARRO'S PERMISSION

"WILL YOU COME with me to the *kraal*, Koma? It's time I pay my respects to the village headman."

"With pleasure, *Mejuffrou*."

They've brought with them ten sacks of maize flour, thirty pounds of salt, three baskets of biltong and lots of tobacco. They leave the Land Rover right outside the village where a bunch of kids, covered in dirt and snot, surrounds them shouting and laughing.

Very spread out and widely separated are little clusters of huts made of sticks and mud with grass roofs. All around, the place is littered with beer bottles and empty cans, old tires, scraps of plastic bags. Past the huts, the bush resumes, crisscrossed with garbage-filled pathways. The traces of western trash are exposed like infected wounds. Zoe retrieves what Dario wrote in his notes: "A little over twenty people live in this permanent settlement. As most of the remaining Bushmen, they too had to give up most of their hunter-gatherer ways."

Koma motions for Zoe to follow him inside the *kraal* as the children help to offload the food.

Narro, the clan headman, is sitting in the shade of a

mopane tree, leaning against its trunk, surrounded by other elders. He is very old, with a heavily lined face and grey peppercorn hair. In contrast with his motionless features, the eyes are still vivid, flickering with life like fleeing gazelles.

Zoe crouches down to shake his hand, with Koma acting as her interpreter.

"I have brought some smoke for you and your people," she says as she hands him three packets of tobacco and lets Koma distribute the rest. The women, who are squatting slightly away from the group of men, also receive their rations.

For a while, they're all intent on filling their bone, metal or wooden pipes, passing around smouldering embers to light them up. Zoe sits cross-legged on the sandy ground, watching them smoking, their tanned, honey-coloured skin glowing in the sunlight. If the metal pipe gets too hot, they roll it quickly between their fingers to cool it down before inhaling and holding the smoke in their lungs, savouring the moment.

The men wear worn-out Western clothes, torn T-shirts and baggy canvas pants; the women sport stained flowery dresses and headbands made of small laced beads. They quietly chat among themselves, laughing a lot, teasing each other, totally relaxed.

They look so at ease, Zoe thinks going back to what Daniel told her the night before in Tsumkwe: "They seem to live on another wavelength. In many aspects their way of thinking is almost alien to ours. They are opportunists, irreverent, strongly egalitarian and value highly personal autonomy. They live in the present, rejoice in their ignorance of the future and have a tendency to unruliness that leads them, at critical moments, to self-destruction."

Zen anarchists, that's what Daniel called them.

❁❁❁

Koma gives her a nod with which he urges her to speak. It's up to her to break the silence.

"My colleague, Dario Oldani, was killed no more than two weeks ago in Johannesburg." It seems almost surreal to talk about it like this using a somewhat official tone, in the desert, in front of a group of Bushmen. She pauses to allow Koma to translate her words into the !Kung language. In the silence that follows, men and women bow their heads. Then, Narro says something and, unexpectedly, everyone grins.

"He knew how to have a good laugh," Koma translates.

Zoe smiles weakly in her turn. She too loved the way Dario treaded lightly on life using humour to break through the invisible barriers people build around themselves. In his diary he underlined twice the Bushman's way of saying: "You can reach the heavens with a belly laugh."

She slowly inhales the hot, desert air before resuming her little speech: "I was allowed to continue my colleague's research out here. We should remain in this area for at least another two seasons. I'm asking your permission to keep our base camp in your *Noré* and use your borehole."

She pauses, waiting for Narro's reply. The act of waiting, in the bush, is everything, a way of life, the salt of any interaction. Like silence: Learning to wield it is among the great arts of living.

The translation of Narro's words reaches her after a long time. "The rain doesn't always come."

She knows that. There have been periods of drought in the Kalahari when it didn't rain for four, five years in a row. And even if it rains, the pans might not get filled with enough water.

"If we have to share the water from the well you must be wise."

No longer free to roam their hunting and gathering grounds, the clan's survival now rests on the borehole. Zoe knows that too.

"We will use the bare minimum," she says, without actually knowing whether *their* notion of bare minimum water consumption might ever get close to *hers*.

With Narro's replies comes also another collective burst of laughter.

"There's no wisdom in showers," Koma translates.

Zoe smiles to herself. *Ja*, our modern weakness: Without our shampoos we cannot be ourselves.

The village chief keeps quiet for a long while.

The children look at her openly, smiling heartily whenever they meet her eyes. The rest of the adults chat softly, apparently unconcerned by her presence in their midst. Still, that broad, carefree smile is on their lips too.

Finally, Narro turns to Koma and speaks to him.

"You can stay," the shaman translates, bending his head towards her.

Zoe nods gratefully. "I thank you, Narro, and your people."

They all know that her request has been a mere formality, that the conservancy in which the *kraal* and the camp stand is managed by the Parks Board, which has already given its approval. Nonetheless, she is keen to acknowledge the Bushmen's right to their land.

There are many silences during this first meeting, interspersed by her words in Afrikaans and their translation into a melodic succession of clicks, but Zoe never feels the urgency to fill those silences. "To see if you get along with people you have to read their silence," Koma told her in one of their first meetings in Schmidtsdrift. She feels at ease in those Bushmen silences. But what about them? What do they read in her silence?

— 16 —

THE INHERITANCE

IN THE FOLLOWING weeks, they find no other remains of the *Australopithecus* skull. Zoe decides to split the workers into two teams: Steve, at the head of the first one, continues to work on the old site, while the other team, headed by Moses, begins to scour the third site identified by Dario.

At times, in the afternoon, she stays behind to clean and analyze the animal fossils that have already been found, collect data and write her notes in the field journal. On a particularly sultry afternoon, too exhausted to continue working, she takes a break and resumes reading Aunt Claire's diary.

Franschhoek, March 10, 1950

Three days ago, on my twenty-first birthday, the postman delivered a parcel addressed to me. Attached was a letter in which the legal executor John Longman notified me that I was the beneficiary of Aunt Charlotte's will. A birthday surprise indeed! I had never met Aunt Charlotte. In the family, pronouncing her name was taboo. I have vague childhood memories of times when I happened to sneak up on women gathered in the kitchen as they talked about her, always in a low voice, furtively. Luckily, Dad was away for work. Mum's reaction was extreme enough. When she found out what the parcel was about, she ordered me to send it back without even opening it. For the first time in my life, I refused to obey. She slapped me in the face. I began to cry and yelled at her that she had no right to do this to me. "You don't know what you're talking about," she said. Grandma came to my aid, trying to calm her. "She's of age now," she whispered. I ran up to my room and opened the package. It contained a silver embossed jewellery box, adorned with coral and turquoise cabochons, which I opened with the small key that I had found along with the cover letter. Inside, there were a gold necklace emblazoned with a teardrop emerald pendant, four gold ingots and a diary, sealed with wax.

Later, I showed mum and grandma the necklace and the ingots (but not the diary). Their curiosity prevailed: They touched those precious objects in wonder, but also with increasing apprehension. We discussed what to do, and decided not to tell dad about the parcel, fearing his wrath.

I didn't dare read Charlotte's diary until late into the night, to be sure everyone was asleep. On the inside of the cover page, I found another letter, a lock of copper-red hair and a picture. I paused on the image: It was the portrait of a beautiful young woman, her eyes looking straight into the camera, aloof. She wore a long, silk dress of the early twentieth century and an eye-catching hat adorned with ostrich feathers. She looked elegant and fashionable. The letter was addressed to me; looking at the date, I realized it had been written when I had just turned six. I copy it here.

Cape Town, March 8, 1930

Dear Claire,

I wish I could see you grow and hold you in my arms. But people's destinies are not always meant to cross each other's paths, although ours are inextricably linked by the family name we bear, as you will learn by reading my diary (please, you need to!). By the time you receive this letter, you will have grown into a graceful and intelligent young lady, full of love for life. And everyone in the family will be proud of you.

What you will read in these pages may sound meaningless to you, hardly credible. Nonetheless, it is true. It will be up to you to decide whether to deny the veracity of this confession or accept it and therefore face your destiny with mature awareness. Your fate—our fate—dictates the solitude of the heart. What I'm trying to tell you in these few lines is that there are many ways to make one's life meaningful and worth living—even without a man's love. Find your way by studying, discovering your artistic talent, caring for others, doing business (ingots, in this case, might come in handy), or, say, by dedicating yourself to a mission or a hobby. Times are changing, even here at the Cape; soon women will be allowed to take care of matters that were once the prerogative of men. I, unfortunately, chose the wrong path. But that's because, after all, I had decided not to live my life. That's why I beg you,

in the name of the love that a distant and unknown aunt feels for you, do not make my mistake. Live your life! Make it a gift from God, as it should be.
Your Aunt Charlotte

The sun is almost close to the horizon now, anxious to break away. Zoe hears the revving and gear-changing of a *bakkie* approaching. The men are back. She closes the journal and puts it into her sack.

— 17 —

BREATH OF THE MOON

ALMOST THREE MONTHS have passed since Zoe's arrival at the camp. Tonight Daniel has joined her and her team for supper, as he often does on his bi-weekly visits to Narro's village. The ranger will spend the night at the camp and head back to Tsumkwe with the first morning light. After they finish their meal, he and Zoe stay up by the campfire, while the others go about their business. So many nights have they sat like this, chatting softly, listening from time to time to the muffled sounds of singing and dancing coming from Narro's village.

"They will dry out with the land," Daniel says in a low voice, gazing towards the Bushmen's huts already wrapped in the shadows of the night. "When they die, a whole way of life will be lost forever. Unrecorded."

The flames crackle softly in the surrounding stillness.

Zoe glances at the ranger before speaking. "Once Koma told me that as much as we might try to write their knowledge in a book, people's souls wouldn't be touched by it."

"He's right. You can't teach it, you've to live it."

The women's chanting rises into the darkness with more insistence, accompanied by rhythmic clapping.

"It's not like the other nights," Daniel says peering into the darkness lurking just beyond the circle of firelight.

Amidst the hand clapping and the female voices, Zoe detects and recognizes another sound: a rhythmic stepping of feet marked by the rattles the men carry tied around their calves.

"It's a trance dance," she says as Sam walks to the fire to pour hot water from the kettle into a mug.

The ranger nods. Then he asks: "Have you ever seen one?"

Zoe shakes her head. "When I was in Schmidtsdrift, from time to time the Bushmen at the camp would stage a healing dance, but they never invited me to attend one."

Sam crouches down by the fire, feeding it. After a while, he brakes the silence and says softly: "That's how they healed me, the Ju/'hoansi."

Zoe looks at him quizzically.

"After the war."

She says nothing. On their first night at Tsumkwe, at the rangers' house, Sam mentioned he had already been to Namibia as a soldier. When, later on, she tried to come back to the subject, he quickly dropped it, leaving her wondering if he too had taken part in the Border War, of which she knows so little. She was still a teenager when the South African army had come up here to fight the Marxist Angolan government and support the counter-revolutionary forces of Jonas Savimbi. The conflict started with a series of covert operations; besides, it was strictly censored. So far, Sam has held back what happened to him in those years. Now, she senses, something seems to have changed in Sam's disposition.

She looks fixedly at Daniel, hoping he too goes radio silent. If no one interrupts him, perhaps this time Sam will tell his story. Again she pays attention to the sounds coming from the *kraal*.

In the distance the women's chanting breathes in and out of the night. Then, as if answering the women's call, Sam sits down and starts talking.

"I was twenty when the Army drafted me," he says, his eyes fixed on the fire, his voice as low as ever. "They sent me to the Namibian border, in Ovamboland, and from there into Angola. The Cubans were now supporting the MPLA's government and South Africa needed to be there to shore up Savimbi."

Sam pauses, puts down the mug, takes the weed pouch out of his pocket and starts rolling a *zol*.

"*Ja*, our proxy war for the democracies of the West," Daniel says, as if trying to prevent silence from taking over. Then he adds, with an undertone of irritation: "They called us *racists*, but we came in handy when the time came to keep the commies in check."

Zoe is taken aback by Daniel's bitter remark. Recollections, again: the angst of those years, when the *rooi gevaar*, the Soviet infiltration into Africa, seemed to meld with the *swart gevaar*, the black danger. It was a toxic mixture for the Afrikaner psyche. The Boers' response was Pavlovian: Leave the *laager*, attack the enemy, ensure the white tribe's survival. And, in passing, save the West's honour.

"That's what our Colonel, Jan Breytenbach, used to say. I mean, the bit about the commies."

"Were you in the 32nd?" Daniel asks, tilting his head sideways to look at the Rasta's face.

"I was."

The ranger looks sternly into Sam's eyes, as if to ensure he's telling the truth. Sam holds his gaze for an assessing moment, then nods and goes back to rolling his smoke.

"I thought one had to volunteer to serve in that unit," Daniel says while Zoe, suddenly shivering, draws a blanket over her shoulders. She still recalls Willem's enthusiastic reaction when news broke of the battalion's operations on the Angolan front.

"If I had to fight then at least I wanted to choose with whom," Sam says. "The 'Buffaloes' were becoming a legend. The Colonel had forged them into a superb fighting machine that scared the shit out of the Angolans. They called them *os terríveis*, the terrible ones. Enough for a young hothead like me to want to be one of them."

He pauses and looks for a moment into the sparkling fire. The scar on his jaw glistens against the dark skin like broken glass.

"It didn't take me long to realize what trouble I had put myself in," he says. "Discipline was inflexible. To enforce it, Breytenbach would even fire on us. On a couple of occasions, he did. His recipe was simple: obsessive training and blind obedience."

Zoe watches Sam's hands, his nimble fingers, the way he deftly adjusts the thin rice paper into a creased, open chute. They don't look like soldiers' hands.

Out there, in the distance, the men's ecstatic dance thumping and the women's rhythmic singing intensifies.

Daniel emerges from his silence: "Most of the soldiers were black, right?"

"*Ja*, mostly Angolans though," Sam replies finally lighting up his *zol*. "Breytenbach had developed a novel approach to guerrilla warfare. Most of the black combatants were captured insurgents who'd been given two options: life imprisonment or medical care, pay and training in return for fighting the MPLA."

"That's what I heard at the time," Daniel says.

"But the devilish genius of that man rests on something else," Sam says as he exhales slowly, letting the smoke out.

Daniel leans forward, his head slightly tilted down, showing the utmost attention.

"While on operations, fighters would use only captured enemy weaponry, wear only enemy military uniforms and boots, consume only enemy rations. Breytenbach wanted us to be utterly untraceable and irrationally feared. And it worked, man."

"So, how come you ended up in that unit?" Daniel asks revealing a hint of doubt in his voice.

"Me and a few other Zulus were odd exceptions. I don't even know why they accepted me in the first place; perhaps because my grandpa and dad had both served in the military. Dad had died in combat."

Zoe watches him again as he draws in the smoke and blows it from his nostrils. In an almost automatic gesture, Sam passes her the smoke and she, for once, doesn't refuse.

"It's the first time I talk about this with Whites, you know," he says looking at her.

She nods, feeling awkward.

Daniel keeps pressing him: "I was told the 32nd didn't follow apartheid rules; is that so?"

"True. Breytenbach was a soldier, a great soldier. He knew that in battle one needs to trust his comrades and commanders blindly. Our commanders were all white, but we ate our rations at the same table, used the same latrines, slept in the same barracks. Pretoria didn't like it, and hard pressed the Colonel to change all that. He never budged, not an inch."

While the smoke of the *dagga* slowly rises into the night, the rhythm of the women's clapping begins to accelerate. Zoe sees the two men listening intently to that far-away call. Tongues of fire light up their rapt faces, throwing hallucinatory shadows against the bush curtain.

After a while Sam resumes his story in a deeper, grimmer tone: "The fear of death morphs you into a different being, you know. All sense of morality goes down the drain."

"But ..." Zoe starts and then falls silent again; what she is about to say has no relevance at all, it's just a clumsy attempt at mitigating the bluntness of Sam's admission. He doesn't even take note. As he talks he keeps rubbing with his left thumb the scar on his jaw—a tic she is by now familiar with.

"You slowly fall prey to a sick frenzy. You develop a lust for blood. You even begin to enjoy killing."

Sam has become unstoppable, as if he too were in a trance. "One day, on our way back to the base camp in the Caprivi Strip after one of our raids into Angola, we showed up at the Namibian border post with the enemy bodies hanging from our combat vehicles." As he speaks he rocks back and forth, his body following the rhythm of his dry, almost hypnotic sentences. "Horrified, the border guards refused to let us pass. Our officer stepped off the reconnaissance tank and put the gun to one of the guards' head, his finger on the trigger: 'Let us through.' I could see the whites of his crazed eyes flash in the dimming light. I was sure that if the guard hadn't caved in, he'd be dead. We passed. Two days later, we passed again. And again. Each time with our load of fresh death."

In the distance, the wild stamping of the dancing men coupled with the rattling of the dry cocoons tied to their calves augments the rhythm of the women's clapping. The healing trance is reaching its peak.

Sam's voice has bewitched her and Zoe wants to hear it again. It's not merely a question of listening to someone who has been in no man's land and has come back. It's something murkier: a subtle lust to learn about the atrocities humans can inflict on one another, to peep into the abyss of violence and see what one can become—what they all might become if they ever fell into it. To keep him talking, she comes up with the silliest of questions: "Did you ever go back home?"

"As little as possible," Sam replies quickly, as if he expected that kind of question to go on with his story. "It was almost worse than being in the bush. When I was there, my mother seemed to cry all the time. She saw what I had become: an animal—*less* than an animal. I'd lie in bed all day, with the shutters shut, drinking beer. If she tried to draw me out of my lethargic state, I'd start screaming. I acted ominously, without restraint; I felt as if something was eating me from the inside out."

Sam pauses, draws in the smoke and slowly blows it towards the black sky, his eyes shut. Then he resumes his story: "I was screaming even in my sleep, reliving gruesome flashbacks over and over. One, in particular, came to me almost every night — the charge of a dead man walking. A zombie. A spectre. A huge Angolan whose belly had been torn by shrapnel; he kept running towards me, shooting at me, with his guts hanging out of his stomach. At times, I wasn't even sure he had ever existed."

Zoe pokes into the embers releasing glimmering red sparks into the night, as if trying to exorcise a hallucination.

"How long did you stay with the 32nd?" Daniel asks.

"Three years. Until one day I tripped over that invisible red line none of us ever mentioned. I broke down, fell apart. I was a total wreck; I cried uncontrollably. I was ashamed of myself. Now they call it PTSD, it sounds less scary. Anyway, they decided to let me go and discharged me from service, but it was too late. I knew I couldn't go home — I'd make everyone miserable. I was suicidal. No one would understand. Plus, I don't like shrinks. I simply don't like them. Instead of going back to South Africa, I followed one of our San trackers to his *kraal* in the Kavango, one hundred fifty kilometres north-east of here. I stayed with his clan for over two years."

"And they cured you," Daniel says.

"That's right."

"How did they do it?" Zoe asks.

"I can't say. Every so often, whenever they felt it was about time, they'd set up a healing dance. Just like that, without notice. They said I had to release the 'arrows of the disease' — that's what they said. Sometimes, between one healing dance and the other, months might pass by. From time to time I would leave to work on a farm near Grootfontein and raise some money to help them out, buy some staple food. Invariably, I would go back to them."

"When did you feel healed?" she asks again, having lost any inhibition by now.

"When the nightmares stopped; when I stopped keeping a loaded .357 next to my pillow; when I realized I no longer woke up in the middle of the night screaming at my soul."

Sam draws from his joint, but it's gone off by now. He takes his time to light it again.

"Don't get me wrong," he says. "Those three years remain an open wound. I still feel anxious in crowds; I still startle at the popping of a toy balloon. But at least now I can cope with it."

The story is over. The three of them keep quiet for a long time, listening to the distant clapping, which has gradually slowed to a subdued, gentle lullaby—as if, musically, the healers and the healed had left the stormy rapids and reached a placid bend in the river. Zoe's mind, instead, is running wildly, looking for ways out, in search of light. When she finally reaches her cot, she struggles to fall asleep.

She thinks of Africa. She was born here, like her ancestors, who lived and died on this continent. It's part of her destiny, she guesses: to be African without wanting to, without knowing how to be African. She loves this land, yet she has closed herself off from the violence in this land. Moreover, the whiteness of her culture—much more than her skin colour—has isolated her from its context. Yes, she was raised as a bush girl, but her head is soaked in Western literature, music, art, science.

During her student years, in that moment of hopeful enchantment allowed by youth, she discovered the sweet seduction of living in Spain, France, Italy. She took part in the research on Neanderthals at the prehistoric Lascaux caves and on Palaeolithic skulls at Monte Circeo. She drank directly at the source from which civil liberties, philosophy and science sprang. Europe lured her with its web of highly cultured, highly sophisticated, highly civilized micro-worlds. How distant Africa had seemed to her, then.

"Yet, you came back," Dario once remarked as they were having coffee on the terrace of her house, their voices floating on the bluish heat haze of the Highveld. Invariably, each round of thoughts brings her back to him. Dario was right, he was always right in reading her unspoken truths. Eventually, her life roots had drawn her back. As the saying goes, you cannot be sown in wildness and settle among daffodils. "In Europe you seemed to have found what you were looking for. What was missing, then?" Dario eventually asked her.

She remembers taking her time before answering, plunging her eyes into the cloudless, limitless eastern plateau beyond the city skyline. "I left my soul at the foot of the Table Mountain. I want it back," she had just heard a returning South African writer tell his interviewee on the morning radio program. She too had yearned for the heart of the land, the immense skies, men pacing over parched plains, the slow passage of time. And the silence—that silence that says it all. She too had romanticized this place. *Her* place. She too had wanted to *feel* at one with life—its pulse, its magic. Instead, turning towards him, she said something else: "I was short of breath, up there."

And if they asked her what she misses most about Europe, now, what would she reply? *Art*, without hesitation. Its intentionality. The processing of the soul. Imagination in motion. But it might not be entirely accurate. Perhaps, even more than that, she misses people intent on questioning life, incessantly scorching and scouring their minds. *That's it.* Two opposite and fascinating worlds have been playing their existential games on her. Attracted to both, she has sought the key to reconcile them without losing anything along the way. But after what happened to Dario, her house of cards has collapsed. Africa, she feels, has betrayed her. Yet only Africa, she knows, can redeem her.

Her life is no different from that of many other white-born children of this continent: She invaded Africa, grew in her womb, was raised by her and learned to love her as if she were her real mother, no matter how dysfunctional the womb might turn to be.

A blue moon looms high up over her—large, pale, mysterious. Zoe remembers how, on one of her first nights at the camp, she found it there, so close, so clean and clear. Eyes wide open in the dark, she followed its slow progress, thinking of all those city people who no longer get to sleep under its silver veil.

From the bush comes the hoarse, rasping cough of a leopard. "It's the only feline that kills for pleasure," Daniel told her during one of their reunions around the campfire. "And if caught in a trap will gnaw off its leg just to be free."

— 18 —

A SHATTERED LIFE

"*EET!* TRY IT!"

Walking briskly ahead of the women's group, Namkwa has found a *tsamma* melon. She has split it in two with her *panga* and is now offering Zoe its white pulp. She hesitantly takes some of it and puts it in her mouth. The bitterness is sickening. Ignoring Zoe's grimace of distaste, the old woman takes a handful of pulp, tilts her head upwards and, holding her hands up over her head, squeezes hard, letting the juice trickle from her skinny fingers into her throat. Taste comes second if you need to quench your thirst in the Kalahari.

For a change, Zoe has joined Namkwa and the women of Narro's clan on a foraging foray into the bush. She follows them into a maze of shrubs having a hard time to keep up with their fast pace. Minute and bare-footed, the San women seem to slide easily through sharp grass and thorn scrub following the invisible paths left by ancient rivers sunk deep into the ground. Some of them have babies tied on their hips, others carry a *karos* on their shoulder, which they rapidly fill with what they collect.

They chat eagerly and hardly stop in their march. If they do, it's to bend and extract from the earth an edible root, a tuber or onion to be cooked in the coals. They accomplish the task with a quick gesture, using a sharp stick or their bare hands. They gather their *veld* food with the self-assurance of an inveterate city shopper, as if they were briskly walking along the aisles of a supermarket, picking what they need, comparing, selecting; fully at ease with their surroundings; finding fulfilment and quietude even in the harshness of their unforgiving land; showing a modern female scientist in their midst what "evolutionary adaptation" de facto means beyond the levity of academic parlance.

Another month slides away. Life in the field may be slow paced, but she makes sure no one—she in the first place—slips into idleness. Day in day out, she has been working with the men at the bottom of a wash. When she stays behind at the camp, she keeps herself busy scraping fossil bones with the three-inch blade of her Swiss Army knife; paying regular visits to the village; studying Dario's notes; writing reports for Kuyper; driving to Tsumkwe with Sam to buy fresh produce, make a few phone calls and have a cup of roiboos with Daniel. Every evening she writes in her field journal. Today, though, she feels ready to make a pause and pick up Aunt Claire's diary again.

Franschhoek, March 30, 1947

No one in the family would tell me anything about Charlotte. "She went down a bad path," they'd just say. "It was so long ago." I felt I needed to speak with Longman, the lawyer; perhaps he would know, perhaps he would tell me the truth. Yesterday I skipped my university classes and went to see him in Cape Town at the address I found on the parcel he had sent me. As I rang the bell at number 22 Kloof Street, just a few blocks away from the courthouse, I didn't get the impression of visiting a law office: The place looked more like a private home, which indeed it was. Mr. Longman, a thin and stooped gentleman well past his sixties, opened the door himself. I didn't expect him to be that old! With his shoulders hunched and his head lolling lamely over his bow tie, he looked more like a beaten dog than an attorney. He had a gaunt, pale face and wore a flannel suit jacket which hung on him as a burlap sack. I introduced myself. He stood in the doorway for a while, visibly puzzled, watching me without saying a word as his face became even paler if that was possible. "You look so much like her," he finally said. He took my hands in his, squeezed them warmly and invited me to come in and have a cup of tea.

After the maid poured our tea and left us alone he told me that, after Aunt Charlotte died fifteen years ago, upon her request he kept the parcel addressed to me until I would come of age. "How did she die?" I asked. It seemed an obvious question, but he looked genuinely bewildered: "Don't you know?" I replied that my family never spoke about my aunt. As for her, she stopped writing in her diary when her betrothed fell from his horse and died. I told him that I wanted to know what happened to her after the incident. He stiffened in his armchair, saying that my family must have had good reasons for behaving the way they did. It was not up to him to reveal certain details about Charlotte's life. He called her by her first name and this led me to believe he knew her very well.

I didn't give up so easily. I argued I had a right to know what happened to my aunt, especially after she had bequeathed me her precious things—including the diary she wrote when she was young, which I considered a very personal gift, something that intimately bound me to her.

Longman looked extremely uncomfortable. He tried to buy time by sipping from his cup of tea. At last he blathered something about finding it hard to talk dispassionately about my aunt. He said that "Miss Charlotte" (this time he added the "Miss" bit) was a very special person ("a wonderful woman, as beautiful as she was intelligent": These were his exact words). I must have looked puzzled. If my aunt was such a special and commendable person why had she been banished from our family? He anticipated my question and embarked on a long explanation about how, considering her station in life, my aunt had made a highly problematic and radically unconventional choice for which he had never fully understood the reason. He then remarked that in those days we, the Du Plessis family, were among the wealthiest and most respected families in the Cape. He kept beating about the bush and I asked him bluntly to get to the point. His answer came as a shock: "Your aunt was a prostitute." He spoke these words looking gently, but firmly, into my eyes, as if in this way—I now assume in retrospective—he could protect her from harsh judgment. I was left speechless. I bet no one dared talk about Aunt Charlotte! In hindsight, this revelation explained many things. I asked him whether he meant my aunt lived in a brothel and he nodded. But he quickly added: "Mind you, she remained a lady. Her clients were carefully selected." I supposed he too was one of the chosen few, and that's what I dared ask him. I had never been so brash, almost impudent. Longman's face, creased with tension, reminded me of curdled milk. He said nothing. I took his silence for a "yes."

Suddenly, I felt anger flushing my cheeks, my neck burning. This woman felt family to me and, in her own way, had tried to help me. Yet, the whole family hid her existence, what she had been. And this man seemed so patronizing. "Why are you all so hypocritical?" I blurted out, unable to contain my frustration. The old man kept quiet for a long while—to give me time to regain my composure, I now suppose. "Yes, I was one of them," he somehow fumbled. Once he recovered his countenance, he told me the whole story. That he was madly in love with her and wanted to be the only one. That him being a widower (he was nearly fifty, she nine years younger) they could have devoted the rest of their days to each other.

"What about my aunt? Did she love you?" I asked him. He was clearly overwhelmed. He mumbled something about being sure of her love for him. "What happened then?" I pressed him. I had to extract from him each single word. "She refused to meet me, even talk to me," he admitted. He started to write her long letters, hoping she would reply. She never did, except

once. The day she killed herself, he got a note hand-delivered by an errand boy. In it she expressed her love for him, but also her fear that her love would be his downfall. Along with the note, she sent the little jewellery box, the ingots and the letter for me. He then told me they had found Aunt Charlotte in her bedroom, bent over her dressing table: She had fired a contact shot to her right temple. Tears ran down his cheeks by this time. I felt moved at the sight of this wrinkled, dignified man whom—now I knew—my aunt had loved so preciously that she wouldn't dare risk his life. He looked like an abandoned puppy, holding to the chain of his pocket watch as if it were a loose leash.

— 19 —
THE CLASH

NO LUCK. THEY keep digging for six months with no luck. At the end of every day Zoe and her team return to the base camp with their shirts drenched in sweat, their hair white from the dust of the salt flats, their nails encrusted with earth. *Fatigue is getting the better of me, of us all.* Three months ago the workers took a break, but she skipped that opportunity, sticking to her original plan. *It was a mistake.* Piet had warned her and was right: *Six months in a row up here are madness.* Now that she too is about to leave, Zoe has to admit to herself she has had enough of the Kalahari. Even going back to the ghosts of her past seems more bearable than having to stand another day in the sweat and the dust.

❁❁❁

Keeping her promise to Narro, Zoe has set tight water-use restrictions at the camp, which she too abides by. Each of them is allowed a basin of water for the morning and evening ablutions and, once a week, a short shower. When it's their turn to take it, the men wash behind the *bakkie*, using an electric pump which sucks water from twenty-five-litre tanks. She, instead, prefers to take the Land Rover and reach the borehole from where the village women pump water manually.

This Friday afternoon she goes off just before sunset, knowing no one else will be there at that time. She lets the hosepipe slip into the borehole and operates the portable motor pump plugged into the vehicle battery.

While she is rinsing her hair, she has a distinct feeling of being watched. Alarmed, she turns abruptly and sees standing in front of her, less than twenty metres away, the most beautiful creature: a mighty male gemsbok, his sabre-shaped antlers shimmering in the sunset's glow. His silhouette stands out against the orange canvas of a sunset sky, making the scene even more striking.

Leaning towards the car through the open door, she manages to turn off the pump motor. She stands there, naked and soapy, watching this marvellous creature, hoping he won't go away too soon. For a long moment, they share the stillness of the desert. Two worlds—the human and the animal—look at each other as if time had been suspended over the horizon. Until the gemsbok lowers his head in a kind of bow, looks at her for the last time and disappears.

She makes her way back to the camp, her hair still wet, dripping water onto her clean shirt, thinking of the sublime and sly ways in which Africa hooks you. *Just when you are about to give up, she reveals herself abruptly, majestically, bewitching you once again.*

Back at the camp, Zoe finds out the men haven't gone to the *shebeen* in Tsumkwe, as they usually do on the weekend. "When they are due back home they try to save drink money," Moses tells her. "They'd rather spend their bucks with friends." Tonight, however, she senses an unusual tension among them. Lately she has felt, almost undetected, an insidious uneasiness running through the camp. Now, suddenly, that menacing mood is coming to the surface. The younger men, in particular, stir restlessly, with jerky movements, like juvenile lions hungry for meat.

The fatigue, the boredom, the isolation in the wilderness: All this has contributed to a dangerous build-up of pressure. She too feels exhausted, easily irritated, frustrated by the sense of failure of her mission—of her entire life, actually. What did she expect to find up here apart from a bag of bones: a new reason to keep living? How have these men kept going all these months?—she now asks to herself—What does failure mean to them?

She too can't wait to get on a bush plane and be shipped, albeit temporarily, home.

Ill at ease, Zoe retires into her tent, avoiding the men's eyes. But she cannot block out their angry voices, which have started lashing mercilessly at each other.

"*Fokkin Zulu*! I'm not your servant." Wally's burst of anger is evidently directed at Sam. Zoe stiffens as she imagines the cook's nostrils flare in the darkness, his eyes no longer smiling and docile, but enraged, like those of a charging buffalo. He has a point: Lately Sam has been assuming a condescending attitude towards the younger team members. She hasn't stepped in quickly enough.

"You and your ilk! Always licking white asses!" Lionel breaks in, his voice hollow and strained.

It isn't just a question of age, power and self-conceit. Sam has made it look like he is on more familiar terms with Zoe and Daniel and this has triggered resentment towards him. Besides, he is a Zulu. In the eyes of many black South

Africans Zulus have been too keen to come to terms with the white regime. Their joining in high numbers the police ranks during apartheid only added to this conviction, even though this circumstance was mostly the outcome of the "divide and rule" approach the Boers leveraged on the several peoples they conquered. Now Zoe imagines Sam's mocking grimace as he takes in those accusations. Still sitting on her cot inside the tent, she freezes, waiting for the inevitable reaction. The Zulu's reply comes like a stab: "Is that what you said to your black brothers as you pushed them into a tire and put them on fire?"

The necklacing. Sam deliberately rubs in their faces one of the most sickening chapters of the black resistance to apartheid: the mob execution of those suspected of being township informants and collaborators of Pretoria's regime.

There is more yelling in *Tsotsitaal*, the creole mix of Sesotho, Zulu, Tswana and Afrikaans spoken in the townships. Zoe can't understand the words being spat loudly at each other, but the sound of what comes next is far too clear: the hoarse, strangulated breathing of men fighting, the mutter of curses, the crashing of crockery, the knocking down of the kitchen stove with its pots and pans. Though terrified, now Zoe runs out of the tent, without the slightest idea of how she could stop the fight. Moses is already beside her. In his right hand, he holds the double-barrelled hunting gun that he always carries with him.

"Leave it to me, *Mejuffrou*."

He fires a single shot upward. And the bush suddenly falls quiet.

Through the halo of the smouldering campfire, Zoe

sees Wally thrown down flat on his back and Lionel massaging his jaw.

Sam looks unscathed. "Just like young bulls," he says, regaining his amused demeanour as Zoe wrings her hands at the scene. "They don't know their place yet."

It's my mistake, she thinks looking at him without smiling. She has been oblivious to what has been happening around her, offending her workers' ethnic pride by showing the weakness of a preference. As if Afrikaners hadn't learned it the hard way. For too long they prayed to a primitive God prone to fomenting divisions among humans by sanctioning racial inequality—besotted, as he allegedly was, with his "chosen" white tribe.

— 20 —

KOMA'S PROMISE

THE MORNING AFTER the fight, cotton-wool clouds fill the blue sky, swaying along, dropping curtseys like damsels in white gowns, as if the landscape itself had decided to make amends for men's insanity.

"We're all tired and ready for a break," Zoe says addressing her team, skipping any preamble. Moses is by her side, rock-solid. "What happened last night should have never happened and must not happen again. It's time to go home, take our well-deserved rest and cool our spirits."

At these words, Sam grins at the congregation, adjusting his wool cap over his ears in his habitual fashion.

She looks sternly at him. "Sam has agreed to stay behind to watch the camp while we're away," she says. "He'll take his break when everyone is back." She pauses. She should reiterate that the success of the whole expedition depends on how well they work together, especially in such a harsh environment. Instead, she says: "We're a good team. You all know that."

The men nod in agreement.

"Nothing of that sort will happen again, Professor Du Plessis," Moses says. "You don't have to worry."

Zoe smiles at her foreman. "I trust your word."

She tries to convey a sense of self-confidence and a hint of poised leadership while, inside, she is still shaking with discomfort.

❁❁❁

Later that day, after she finished updating her field journal, Zoe crouches close to Koma outside his hut, by the fireside. Spending time in the open bush with him has taught her many things. Not a day goes by that this old man, wrapped in his wrinkly skin, doesn't give proof of his being at one with his surroundings. What most intrigues her, though, are his powers as a shaman—a healer.

"*Oom*, what does it mean when they say a black shadow is walking behind a person?"

She has meant to ask him this question for some time now, but she has been stalling. The next day she'll be leaving for Johannesburg with the rest of the crew and, before she leaves, she wants to know.

"It means the soul of this person is starving."

"At the village, they think a black spirit is following me. That's what Sam heard. Is that so?"

Koma looks into the dusk, as the last light of day drains from the sky.

"I can see it too. It was already with you in Schmidtsdrift."

"You never told me about it."

"There's a time when words come out by themselves. We must wait for it."

Zoe falls silent, poking at the small fire in front of them. *Does this mean Koma knew about the curse all along?* Then she realizes the absurdity of her thoughts.

She watches the shaman's face glow in the fire's halo for a little longer then she ventures to ask: "Do you think you can cure me, *Oom*?"

"Only the sky can tell."

She closes her eyes, breathes in the night air and holds it in for a long time, imitating the San's way of smoking their pipes. When she opens her eyes again she meets the old man's gaze.

"Once you're back, we'll try," Koma says.

It's a promise.

— 21 —

BACK HOME

THE BUSH PLANE takes off from the dirt track on the outskirts of Tsumkwe. Instinctively, Zoe turns towards the small window. She lets her view drift away, afloat the sea of sun-burned grass. The ashen light pours down on hundreds of termite mounds, rising from the earth like fingers pointed against the gods. She keeps staring out till the scene outside recedes faster and faster into the distance. Then she looks down to examine her hands, scratched by the thorny bushes, and fingernails, cracked and still lined with dirt. She is going to the Department empty-handed. What's worse, her physical exhaustion hasn't eased the pain in her heart. The void left by Dario can't be traded in.

She runs her fingers through her hair and feels its roughness. Her throat tightens in self-commiseration. She is about to cry, find temporary relief in her tears. But no, she won't. She swallows hard and looks once again out of the small window. *All this emptiness.* She thinks of her diggers, who will soon go back with her into *this* desert, and of Sam, still *out there.* "You'll find the camp spick-and-span when you're back, *Mejuffrou,*" he said while driving them to the landing strip that morning.

❁❁❁

The bush plane left Zoe and her team at the airport in Windhoek. There, they've taken an international flight to Johannesburg. The plane approaches the city flying over the treeless squalor of Alexandra, a dirty mess of zinc sheeting and coal-fire smog. Past the black township, there come the ostentatious towers of Sandton City and the leafy streets of the northern white suburbs. From the window Zoe makes out villas and cottages plunged in the greenery of gardens and lawns surrounded by high walls and electric fences. The blue reflections of hundreds of swimming pools punctuate the scene: Dario once listed them among "the conspicuous markers in the geography of privilege." Here she is, then, back to *eGoli*, its rapacious nature. But after the stark desolation of the Kalahari even this place of greed and misery seems, by contrast, to wreathe in glory.

Upon landing, the city glistens neat and formal in the sun after a sudden shower. It takes the taxi twenty minutes to take Zoe from the airport to Melville, her suburb: a place straddling white and black, rich and poor, order and chaos. "A snapshot from South Africa's future," as Dario once described it. She has never thought of it this way, but indeed it's a border area, a frontier in the frontier zone.

Zoe steps out of the taxi and stands for a while in front of her house, looking at it as if she's seeing it for the first time. It's a modest, single-storey bungalow with a corrugated tin roof like the local farmsteads. She grabs her backpack and climbs the steps to the *stoep*. The hibiscus shrub near the entrance door is overgrown, hiding most of the nearby window; she stops to watch its scarlet flowers flutter in the light breeze, dancing away with sad sweetness.

Once inside, Zoe wanders through the house finding traces of a life sunk away. She feels like an intruder there, peeping into the privacy of someone else's life. She enters the master bedroom. The objects on the dressing table might as well be samples in a private museum: a pair of horn combs, half-spent hair lotions, a small bottle of clove fragrance. From the window, the skyscrapers of the CBD loom into the shimmering light like giant baobabs, steely and unmoved. Only the shrill cries of the hadedas break the silence.

She undresses, steps into the bathroom and takes a long, hot bath. Before quickly blow-drying her hair she turns on the heater. It's a mild mid-winter day yet she can't dispel the shivers running through her body. The fridge is empty. She finds a frozen pizza in the freezer and heats it up in the microwave oven, then switches on the kettle to make coffee. In this urban silence, the buzz of electric appliances has an almost comforting effect.

A few hours later, as she's dozing off on the sofa, the phone rings.

It's her brother.

"At last! I've been trying to get in touch with you all morning. At the Department, they told me you were on your way. When will you be here?"

"What?" she asks, slightly annoyed. She just got home, dead tired, and doesn't get the point of her brother's rushed questioning.

"Oh, come on! You forgot!"

"Forgot what?"

"The grand reception to celebrate the Finistère's tricentennial. It's tomorrow night!"

"*Ag*!"

"Can't believe that. Zoe, I even sent you a reminder about it in my last letter!"

"*Ja*, but I didn't realize ..."

Zoe senses her brother's irritation and, under it, his anxiety.

"Listen," he says. "You *got* to be here. In the invitations we sent out you appear as the godmother of the evening. We spoke about it the last time you called me from Tsumkwe, remember?"

"Did I *really* agree to that? Honestly, André, you know I'm not cut out for this kind of thing."

"It's only a question of shaking hands with some VIPs," he says, the irritation in his voice giving way to a mellow tone. "Just a few words, no more than the ones you'd share with your Bushmen friends. You wouldn't have time to do more in any case. There'll be four hundred guests."

"Oh gosh!"

"You can't let me down, *ousus*," he says, his voice now down to a whisper.

He has a point. He's managed the family's business for years while she devoted herself to her studies, her *useless* research. *I can't let him down.*

"Well, then," she finally says, "I'll take a flight in the morning. I hope I'll still find a seat."

She hears him release a deep breath and then laugh.

"Ah! I knew I had to stay ahead of the game! It's all set. Your ticket is waiting for you at the SAA counter. You're on the 9:05 a.m. flight."

André's sigh of relief is unequivocal. She can picture his jubilant smile on the other end as he leans back and lights a cigarette.

"You just need to buy yourself the most gorgeous evening dress. Splash the cash: It's on me. I know how stingy you are when it comes to shopping for clothes."

"No need. And, by the way, shops will be closing soon. I'll look into mum's wardrobe."

"If I'm not mistaken, mum's dresses never fit you."

"This time they will. Courtesy of the Kalahari."

— 22 —

THE GREEN DRESS

AS THE PLANE descends towards Cape Town, the sun and the western coastline of South Africa rise roughly in tandem from the passenger windows. As usual, the pilot heads to the south of the airport before turning back to land, so that, as he approaches the coastline again, the incoming tourists are granted a view of one of the world's most stunning intersections of land and water. There is nothing quite like the sight of Table Mountain emerging from a bed of clouds, with the city spreading at its feet until it finds the ocean.

Zoe overhears the comments of the American couple sitting by her side: "Isn't it absolutely gorgeous!" "And look at this light! Amazing!" They sound so enthusiastic. She wonders if their optimism will take a blow once they leave the airport and drive into town past the dreariness of informal settlements.

❁❁❁

"You're as skinny as a string bean!" André cries as he grabs Zoe by the waist and swings her around in the middle of the arrival hall.

"I've been sweating for six months."

"How did it go, by the way?" he asks taking her bag. "Did you find the skull that will grant you your minute of celebrity?"

Suddenly that lump in her throat again.

"Let's not talk about it," she replies, looking away.

"Then let's talk about tonight," her brother hastily says walking out of the airport. The brusque change of subject startles her; but, obviously, what mostly matters to him now is *the damned party*. After a while, as they reach the parking lot she asks, somewhat reluctantly: "How's it coming along?"

"Fine, I guess." Then, as he holds the car door open for her, he says: "Cyril's help has been invaluable."

For a while they drive quietly across the plain towards the blue mountains, in a landscape filled with clapped-out cars and squatter shelters. With their silence, Zoe feels they are paying their respects to that "disposable" part of humanity hidden behind rags and corrugated metal walls.

"What about the old grumpy Afrikaners of the valley?" she asks, eventually breaking the spell. "Will they attend too?"

"Most of them, except for some diehards. And for Willem, of course—he took it badly."

"Can't be much of a surprise."

"You never quite liked him, although you never wanted to tell me why," André says reaching out to find his sister's hand. "I wonder if this time I was able to serve your revenge on a silver platter."

"It would still be a bitter serving," she says, her eyes fixed on the road. "There is no relief in revenge."

She, at least, didn't feel any relief when, having just turned eighteen and obtained legal control over the estate, faced Willem to warn him to stay away from Georgina.

❁❁❁

The drive takes them less than an hour. As they roll through the driveway to the Finistère, Zoe notices that two rows of torches have been placed along the hedges. At night they will produce the intended dramatic effect: the feeling of stepping into some gracious tale. The area in front of the main entrance has been decorated with banks of red roses and white camellias: passion and virginity—a bold, almost decadent juxtaposition. She doesn't recognize her brother's hand behind it.

She enters the banquet hall and tries to imagine how it will look within a few hours, by nightfall: It will be a sparkling of crystals, a romantic flickering of candles—like in mom's time. The satin-lined sofas have been pushed against the walls and a small orchestra has been set up on a raised platform. In the smaller adjacent room, Zoe parades along the bartenders' corner and the refreshment tables. Here and there bouquets of white lilies and roses, matching the pallid colour of the candles, have been arranged in tall, elegant glass vases.

"Did we overdo it?" André asks, joining her in the middle of the hall after having imparted some instructions to the catering manager.

"This needs to be an unforgettable evening, right?" Zoe replies, her eyes still fixed on the white lilies.

"Yes, I did it on purpose: a homage to bygone innocence," her brother says following her gaze.

"I never thought you could be such an aesthete! Anyway, tonight he will be the real touch of colour, the Black Prince. Where've you hidden him, by the way? In the cellar?"

"Close. He's doing one final check on the wine list. You'll meet him later," André says raising both his arms and crossing them behind his head as if to stretch himself. It's one of those gestures Zoe likes most in him: It conveys such irrepressible confidence in himself and the world.

"You should get some rest. I bet you're no longer used to staying up."

"I never was. And still can't understand why I'm here."

"A bit of socializing can only do you good," he says ruffling her short hair. "You're running the risk of turning into a fossil yourself."

Before repairing to her room Zoe goes to greet Georgina. She too is excited and busy with the preparations. "We haven't had a party like this since your father's best times." She doesn't hide her disappointment, though. "A black man at the head of the Finistère. I never thought we'd come to this."

"You should be happy, Georgina. Things are changing, and not just because you can now cast your vote in the elections."

"For us Coloured, nothing will change. Before, we were too dark; now, we aren't dark enough."

Zoe looks at her *aia* endearingly, assessing her words. *She may well have a point. Racism is in the eye of the beholder.*

"Can't believe how mean they are to their black brothers and sisters," Georgina says, venting her frustration. "Especially to those who come from other countries: you know, Mozambique, Congo, Zimbabwe, Malawi."

Zoe nods sadly. The cab driver who earlier had driven her to the airport was adamant in accusing black immigrants of stealing jobs and women from local Blacks.

"They beat them and burn their shacks," Georgina says

scrubbing the kitchen table for the umpteenth time. "They should be ashamed of themselves. They're no better than the white *baas.*"

"Don't get so wound up, *Ouma*, it's bad for your health," Zoe says as she hugs her and changes the subject. "Are mother's evening dresses still in her wardrobe?"

"*Ja*, always been there. You should've told me you wanted to wear one of them, though. I could have aired them out for you. You'll smell of camphor."

"I can't expect to smell like a fresh rose. André is right, I have almost become a fossil myself. I can still be introduced as the 'ancient' sister dug up from an old closet."

It has been a long time since Zoe entered her parents' room. White linen sheets cover each piece of furniture; the whole place is wrapped in a shroud that still no one dares to touch. She opens the big wardrobe and runs her hands along a hedge of multi-coloured silk interspersed with clouds of chiffon, damask and ostrich feathers. She buries her face in it, hoping in vain to find mom's scent, lost forever amidst the heavy notes of camphor, suffocated by that pedantic, anaesthetizing way of storing the past.

She chooses a memory: a long, forest-green silk gown with an open back, to be worn with a matching pair of gloves that reach above the elbows. Then she lies down on the bed, imagining herself to be still a little girl allowed to crawl up under the covers between mom and dad on a Sunday morning. Tiredness soon has the upper hand and she slides into a colourless sleep, adjusted to the room's aura.

❁❁❁

It's Georgina who wakes her, a few hours later, softly knocking on the door.

"Am I late?" Zoe asks in alarm.

"No rush. But I figured you'd fall asleep without putting on an alarm clock. Do you need any help?"

"*Nee*, thank you. I just need to freshen up."

Zoe goes to her room and takes a shower. She then fixes her hair as best as she can before slipping on the dress she has chosen. She looks at herself in the mirror: It fits her, although she finds it uncomfortably revealing. For a moment, her mom's face—with her haughty, slightly bored look—appears over hers; for the first time she seems to be able to understand this young woman, *too young*. Caught in a world to which she didn't belong and despite her unhappiness, this woman tried to love her and her brother as best as she could.

Before leaving the room, Zoe draws from Aunt Claire's jewellery box the necklace with the pendant that their ancestress Charlotte bequeathed to her niece. She looks into the mirror again. The emerald drop perfectly matches the gown's colour and her eyes. To no purpose, she sadly realizes.

As she comes down the last of the stairs, Zoe meets Cyril's smile. He goes to her solicitously and kisses her gloved hand.

"You look wonderful, Zoe."

She feels his approving gaze on her and for a moment basks in it.

"Thank you, Cyril. I haven't had a chance to congratulate you on your new position. Welcome to the Finistère."

"I'll try my best to live up to the trust you and André have honoured me with."

"I'm sure you will," she says, glancing at the flawless white of his tuxedo.

"Always so annoyingly impeccable, aren't I?" he says in a self-mocking tone, correctly interpreting her thoughts again.

André interrupts them in time to relieve her from the need to find a witty answer.

"*Ousus*! What a transformation, from a trilobite to a nymph!" Then he says quietly, his lips close to her ear: "You look just like mom."

Zoe glances at him and sees his eyes are suddenly moist.

"Well, are we ready for the show?" Cyril asks.

André resumes his composure and turns to their partner. "Now or never ..."

Cyril leans forward in a theatrical bow and then makes a courteous gesture inviting brother and sister to proceed to the banquet hall. Zoe doesn't miss the knowing look the two men exchange, but just then her attention is diverted by a buzzing sound of voices. The first guests have arrived.

— 23 —

THE THIEF OF STORIES

IN THE TWO hours that follow Zoe smiles, shakes hands, sips champagne, forces herself to take part in conversations that convey nothing of interest to her, but that people seem to enjoy utterly. André introduces her to bankers, diplomats, landowners, businessmen, corporate executives—all of them accompanied by wives, girlfriends or unofficial lovers who need to be pleasantly and lavishly entertained. For the first time, she also comes into contact with members of the new black elite.

Regardless of her interlocutors' standing or skin colour, though, Zoe realizes she doesn't have any light conversation topics to throw around like sparkling gems. For years she hasn't been doing much else than working with fossils and engaging in speculations concerning human evolution. In the last six months, she hasn't once gone to the movies, watched TV, attended a theatre performance, read newspapers—there's a whole world out there to which she no longer feels she belongs.

Yes, on her flight back to Johannesburg she read the news that De Klerk's Afrikaner National Party left the government of national unity, while, albeit recalcitrant, the Zulu leader Mangosuthu Buthelezi is still supporting the

Xhosa President Nelson Mandela. Yet, when earlier on André made some comments about the latest political developments, the only thing she was able to think of was that perhaps now her workers would have one less reason to fight.

Luckily, André and Cyril have set up things to run smoothly, and this helps her social inadequacy to go unnoticed. Indoors, a small ensemble is playing evergreen dance songs; outdoors, on the lawn facing the west wing, a video projector is churning out scenes from vintage movies. "Modern Times!" "Some like it Hot!" "Clark Gable!" "Audrey Hepburn!" cry out the guests gathered in front of the big screen as they compete in guessing movie titles and identifying lead actors.

Around eleven, Cyril approaches her. "Would you have a minute? I'd like you to meet a dear friend of mine."

"I'm afraid I've run out of moves for tonight ..."

He offers her his arm and leads her to a corner where a man facing away from her is talking to a middle-aged couple.

"Kurt, let me introduce you to the godmother of the evening, Miss Zoe Du Plessis, a renowned paleoanthropologist. Zoe, this is Kurt Van der Merwe, our celebrated writer."

The man turns to greet her. In front of her stands the thief of stories. She stares at him, speechless: on his lips, the same slightly mocking smile; only his gold-rimmed eyeglasses are missing.

"How unexpected," she murmurs, suddenly realizing why his face looked somewhat familiar when they met at the Drostdy. How could she not recognize the bard of the *volk*, the Afrikaner poet who in her youth every Boer would die for? But then he turned political, started to criticize the apartheid regime and got imprisoned …

"It was written in the desert sand we'd see each other again, *Mejuffrou*," Kurt says stretching out his hand.

"Apparently, you've already met," Cyril says with a small note of disappointment in his voice.

"Just the time of a cigarette in the night," the writer says, looking intently at her.

"Zoe," Cyril goes on quickly recovering his poise, "let me also introduce you to Zelda and Steve Gordon. They finally decided to pay us a visit."

"And what better occasion than this one!" Zelda cries showing her perfect teeth. "Such a fabulous party!"

"Just to give you the whole picture," Cyril says for Zoe's sake, "Zelda and Steve are our biggest wine importers from the East Coast."

She shakes hands, smiling faintly at the two well-fed, well-dressed, overly self-confident Americans. She remains silent, though, still bewildered by the renewed encounter with the stranger from Graaf-Reinet.

"We were talking about Africa," Zelda says, coming to her rescue with the typical savoir-faire of those accustomed to doing public relations and filling uneasy silences. She is a small and heavily tanned woman in her mid-forties, swathed in an elaborate periwinkle dress.

"We were wondering why we Westerners are so irremediably drawn to this continent," her husband says, looking at ease in his sporty bearing—as if life were a well-established series of court games.

Greed, perhaps? Zoe tells herself, but refrains from open comments—too predictable, by the way, and too polemical.

"*Ex Africa semper aliquid novi,*" Kurt answers for her, putting his hands back in his pockets. "There is always something new out of Africa, argued Pliny the Elder." He has a deep voice, but the tone is dismissive, laconic, like the one often used by British men of good standing. He speaks English with no apparent accent, Zoe now notices.

The couple exchanges a puzzled look: Kurt's lofty cultural remark has momentarily silenced them. Zelda, however, doesn't give up. Waving a hand in the air with her long, red-lacquered fingernails, she says to no one in particular: "Actually, I meant something different. The East can either charm you or leave you indifferent. But when one gets to Africa ... this place really gets under your skin, doesn't it?" She stops abruptly, looking at Kurt's blank expression, realizing she has been talking too much.

"*Le mal d'Afrique*, here it is again," Cyril says. "We owe it to you writers this bestselling idea of white man's nostalgia for Africa."

"I couldn't agree more," Zelda's husband says, happy to have found some common ground.

All this time, Zoe has been watching Kurt's eyes. Their slate gray-blueness contains a sombre, almost metallic shade, like skies about to quickly cloud over. And, like the first time, she senses they harbour an unspoken sadness. Just then, the writer slightly tilts his head towards her, making a swift gesture with his left hand as if to dismiss Cyril's comment.

"Let's hear from Professor Du Plessis instead," he says lifting his glass of red wine towards her. "She is the real expert here, and not only because of her field of study; from what I gather, her family tree is deeply rooted in this continent."

Zoe stiffens at the mention of her family's past. After a moment of awkward silence, she turns to the couple and tries to speak as amiably as possible: "Well, none of us gets easily away with our ancestral origins. They're part and parcel of what we are as humans."

"Damn all those poor anthropomorphic apes," Cyril says, wrapping an ironic tone in one of his bright smiles.

"I guess we come to Africa like teenagers still in search of their moorings," Zelda says.

"Or better, like adopted children looking for their biological makers," her husband says.

"Somehow," Zoe says choosing to go along with the couple's rather bland remarks. "We now know we were inside Africa's womb some immemorial time ago. That's why we can't walk past her as if she never existed. Instinctively, we feel it's here where we truly belong—at least as a species."

"Nice," Kurt says. "A wee bit rhetorical, perhaps."

"Perhaps," she admits looking sternly at him. "But I guess it's in our nature to try and create a grander narrative of our story."

"And Africa can provide a most memorable script. Like in the movies," Kurt says without concealing a tinge of sarcasm.

"You're not fair here, my dear friend," Cyril says in a merry tone, trying to curb Kurt's mordancy. "'To know ourselves we have to run through Africa's psychic tunnel.' Isn't that what you once said?"

"Right. We won't know Africa until we get to fear it. In pain and terror."

Zoe senses the situation has taken on surreal tones. Five people, apparently with very little in common, are busy constructing or deconstructing Africa. She nods at the two Americans who are watching her graciously, grateful for her words. She can't be dismissive of those who seek to understand Africa, even when they look at it through the mystique of a continent. She doesn't despise foreigners who land here in search of a dream, a romantic idea to be grasped over a hasty holiday. True, they arrive wearing well-ironed khaki shirts, big game hunting boots, explorer binoculars, and most of the time they seem to leave without many more clues than they came with.

But the Whites who "stayed," sometimes generation after generation, are no better—only more cynical, disaffected, or embittered by what lurks beneath the surface, behind the umpteenth magic sunset on the savannah. If those Whites want to dream, to break free—even momentarily—from the burden of their African lives, they fly away. They go to London, Rome, Paris, New York, to be in the midst of people who, in their own way, are disillusioned and cynical. She calls it the symmetry of disenchantment. Sure, it doesn't happen to all of them, but it happens. Frequently enough.

"We read in the newspapers that white South Africans are leaving the country *en masse*," Zelda says, changing the subject. "Is that something you too are thinking about, Mr. Van der Merwe?"

Zelda's husband shoots a dirty look at his wife for her lack of tact.

"I don't think so," Kurt replies wearily. "For once, I might just go with the flow and watch the insanity of it all. At my age, I guess I've earned the right to simply be a political voyeur. As I said, we Africans are masters at putting up unforgettable shows."

Again, Zoe doesn't miss the sarcasm in his reply.

"Sorry to interrupt, Kurt; if you don't mind, I'd like to introduce our friends here to the new mayor," Cyril says, gently pushing the couple away as he scowls at him. Kurt returns his friend's glance with an expression of mock contrition.

Now that they're alone, Zoe has the impression whatever she says will be the wrong thing. Yet, she doesn't want to behave like those women who in front of a famous writer abdicate their power of speech. Unlike her, *he* is famous, and with an exemplary personal story to look up to.

"Are you always so abrasive with people you don't like?"

"What makes you believe I don't like you?"

She looks awkwardly at her arms folded across her stomach as if they could protect her from this man's brazenness.

"You well know I was referring to the Americans."

"Africa is something different and you know better than I do. They wouldn't like Africa so much if, after a day of safari, they couldn't take a proper shower."

Zoe glances down at her glass and smiles feebly.

"You know what it feels like talking to you?"

"You tell me."

"That naiveté is a crime. And whoever shows it doesn't deserve your sympathy."

As they talk, she is able to observe him. Even though Zoe wears high heels, he's a half-head taller than her. His ashen-streaked hair is cut very short; only his forelock is kept long and seemingly ungovernable, concealing, though partially, a scar running sideways across his forehead. His jaw protrudes rather unnaturally below a sharp and sun-scorched nose almost as thin as his lips. He wears a very short, well-trimmed beard and moustache of a dusty dun colour. The left corner of his mouth seems to be permanently turned down, conveying that peculiar air of covert sarcasm. *What a formidable shield.*

"I'm sorry I didn't recognize you at the Drostdy. Besides, I'm ashamed to admit I don't remember reading any of your books," she says.

"Unforgivable."

"Still writing in the desert?"

He takes his time to answer, licking his lower lip with the tip of the tongue.

"Not *in* the desert. But *of* deserts. Moral deserts. It's a story about shame."

Zoe shrugs involuntarily, looks around and sees André gesturing to join him.

"Excuse me," she quickly says indicating her brother. "I guess I'm not done with introductions yet."

"You must be missing your safe cocoon in the Kalahari," he says with a half bow.

She briskly crosses the room to join André and his guests.

"Zoe," André says putting his arm around her waist, "let me introduce you to the Director of FirstRand Bank in Cape Town."

As she smiles amiably at the new guests, she feels she's slowly slipping away, as if trapped in a water bubble. She sees people open and close their mouths but can't make out what they are saying. She's still thinking about the writer, the way he seems to gain access to people's minds.

Later, Cyril approaches her again.

"Kurt is rather moody. I hope his ways didn't make you

run away; that's what usually happens with him, especially if it's women."

Zoe turns towards him with a knowing smile. "Still trying to save him from himself?"

"A lost cause," Cyril says with a snort.

"Have you known him for long?"

"We grew up in the same house. My mother was the family's maid."

The lights have been dimmed. The couples are gliding across the old wooden floor, which groans in annoyance. Zoe leaves the room and heads for the garden, strolling across the lawn. The screening area is deserted. She sits on a nearby bench, leaning her elbows on her knees, face propped on her hands, and watches that memorable scene in *Casablanca*: "Play it, Sam. For old times' sake." The footage stops as Bogart—impeccable in his smoking suit, a cigarette dangling from the mouth—stares into his memory.

"The inevitability of fate and the pain of love renounced," Kurt says. He's standing in the darkness not far from her, Zoe realizes with a little start.

"Love lived as a sacrifice rather than as a possession," she says feebly.

She sees his shadow moving closer and then the white starched cuff of his dress shirt. He's offering her a smoke. She declines with a slight shake of her head. When Kurt flicks the lighter for his cigarette, Zoe's emerald pendant becomes alive.

"A teardrop from the sea. Very beautiful."

"I inherited it. From a woman considered to have loose morals, to put it mildly."

"A soft spot for a bad seed?"

"Not brave enough to be one, perhaps."

She bites her lip. What's she doing? Why is she revealing herself like this?

He lets her off the hook, leading the conversation towards less slippery surfaces.

"Cyril had started telling me about your expedition to the Kalahari, but we were cut short."

"There's not much to say. Not much luck, thus far."

"It mustn't be easy for you up there."

She shudders, thinking back to the fight among her workers, but doesn't say anything.

"How long are you planning to be in your desert?"

"Well, as Professor Kuyper says, until I haven't found my ... *Homo*."

She hears him break into a laugh.

"One thing I've learned for sure," she says. "How easy it is to retreat from the world and how difficult it is, then, to return to it. Tonight, people were quoting movies, TV programs, new book titles, their kids' favourite pop songs, and I felt left out. An alien."

Kurt keeps quiet.

Talking about herself again, sharing her feelings. *What a mistake.*

"How silly of me, telling you such things, after what you've been through ..."

Even in the semi-darkness, Zoe feels him stiffen, but she pretends not to notice. Going against her nature as she did with Sam in the Kalahari, she forces herself to ask the question.

"What did you miss most when you were … well, you know, when you were behind bars?"

The silence becomes even thicker. Were it not for the red glow of the cigarette, Zoe might be led to believe that the thief of stories is gone. Until, finally, she hears his low, laconic voice again: It seems to come from distant lands, even though he's no more than a few feet from her.

"The sea. Its smell, its salt on my skin. I never swam so much as in those seven years in jail. Every day I imagined myself doing a steady, slow crawl, theoretically endless, with the ocean yawning at me from below. I practised that mental swimming like a Zen monk, almost in a state of trance."

"The sea as a black masseur," she murmurs, trying to remember the exact title of a book Dario gave her to read.

"*Haunts of black masseur: The swimmer as hero*," Kurt says, coming to her aid. "An unconventional read. I'm impressed."

Now that the screening has come to an end, the music flows clear and sweet out of the dance hall, along with the clinking of glasses and the soft chatter.

"I suppose all this seems to you disarmingly banal," she says, making a vague gesture towards the ballroom, the orchestra, the flower arrangements, the candle lights.

"Not necessarily. Beauty and lightness have their advantages."

"Even when they border with superficiality?"

"Prison taught me a lot, including things I wouldn't want to learn. Helplessly witnessing torture, death, the loss of human dignity, the abyss of bestiality our fellow humans can fall into. All this destroys something inside you—something that shouldn't even be touched. That's when superficiality shows its benefits. It can even prove cathartic."

Kurt inhales his cigarette deeply; in the incandescent glow, she catches a glimpse of the writer's troubled expression. He too has exposed himself. He too regrets it.

The band is now playing "Killing me softly."

Another long silence between them, as they both listen to the music.

Kurt's voice reaches her almost in a whisper: "Would you care to dance?"

Asking this question must have cost him considerable effort, she senses. *How would he take no for an answer?* For a moment, the gnarled confidence with which he seems to keep his life under control cracks and Zoe peers, unseen, into his loneliness.

She won't dance with him, she will decline the invitation politely. The party is almost over, only a few of André's friends will stay behind. The thief of stories will soon be gone too and, most likely, she will never see him again.

But she doesn't say no. And when he gently takes her hand, she doesn't stop him. He leads her out of the grass and onto the tiled terrace, close to the music, then turns. She leans towards him and they drift together into that sad song. His hand presses slightly against her back; she follows this invitation and lets her body adhere to his, feeling his nervous tension as if it were a second invisible skin. He tilts his head towards hers, almost touching her cheek. She feels the music waving through her conscience as she dances with this famous stranger, a thief of stories who worships ocean swimming.

The song is over.

He holds her there for one long moment. Then he lets her go.

Extending her gloved hand, Zoe hastily takes leave of him. She is eager to go back to her desert, preferring its desolate harshness to the danger she has just shunned.

— 24 —

SONGS OF THE SIRENS

After the official announcement that Cyril Kunene was made a partner of the Finistère, the estate has been stormed by local and foreign reporters. Everyone, it seems, wants to interview and photograph the first black businessman who has managed to make inroads into this historic stronghold of Afrikaner power: the Cape winelands. André, too, gets dragged into the whirlwind of interviews, phone calls and public appearances. At one time, overwhelmed, he tries to engage Zoe as well. But she is adamant: He can't ask more of her public persona. When the press guys are about to arrive, she invariably slips away, burrowing herself into the reading room or taking Jolly for long rides.

With a contrasting mix of fascination and loathing, reading to Georgina the statements Cyril and André give to the newspapers has become a daily pastime. In truth, anything is better than having to prepare a less than exciting report for Professor Kuyper.

"Listen to this, *Ouma*. from the *Cape Argus*: 'When I was a buyer in the U.S., I refused to taste South African wines,' Kunene says. 'I waited for the fall of apartheid and the liberation of Nelson Mandela to acknowledge their dignity in the free market.'"

"What a loudmouth!" Georgina cries. "If it weren't for men like your grandfather or great-grandfather, he wouldn't even know what wine is and where it comes from ..."

Zoe smiles feebly at her *aia*'s comment. For so long has she tried to strip any sense of honour from her ancestors' past. But the Afrikaners have been called in front of History's tribunal, at last. And they have pleaded guilty. The infamous deeds and barbarous injustices for which they are responsible will be righted. If not totally, at least partially. Most of all, publicly. And rightly so. Only a long, excruciatingly honest, cathartic journey will set her people free from a shameful past. But now that the age of atonement has begun, that her *volk*'s wrongdoings will be exposed and purged, she can allow herself to feel a hint of pride for what those early Huguenots in the Cape and their descendants were able to accomplish.

She leafs through the pages of another newspaper.

"Here is André's interview to *Business Day*: 'We shall export most of our production. The best restaurants in the world, from Lespinasse in New York to Clarke's in London, already include in their wine list a Pierre Jourdan Brut or a Glen Carlou Chardonnay. Both wines are produced from grapes grown in the only wine region on the planet that enjoys the breezes of two oceans. The vineyards that have put Franschhoek, Stellenbosch, Paarl, Constantia on the map of great wine regions would never grow without their moist breath. Being the oldest of the New World wine countries, South Africa has the potential to compete with Californian and Australian wines.'"

"Are you making fun of us, *ousus*?" André catches her by surprise walking into the kitchen followed by Cyril. The two men are beaming with self-satisfaction. *Like the sun and the moon—different, yet somehow complementary.*

"More than winemakers you look like pop stars," she says.

"It's marketing, my dear," André says, stealing her last biscuit.

"You should be pleased with him, Cyril. The kid is learning quickly."

"No doubt," he says as he leans forward with both hands on the edge of the table, slightly tilting his head to peer at the title of the book lying among the newspapers. His forearms shine smooth and vigorous under the rolled-up sleeves of his white shirt.

"I see you're reading my friend Kurt."

"It's the least I can do, after letting on I had never read his work."

"Well, what do you think of his writing?"

"I've only gone through three of his books so far ..."

"Enough to get an idea. Go ahead, I can bear criticism on his behalf."

"Ruthless. Bleak."

"He certainly doesn't spare anyone. Not even himself."

"Evocative, nonetheless. Such a contrast: the dreariness of his stories, the hideous truths, and the luminous quality of his wording. As if the only hope for salvation lay in a perfectly crafted sentence. In that austere beauty."

"Once I heard a critic say that some of his passages can produce little awakenings. Let's not forget he's above all a poet. Though Kurt says very few people nowadays would stop and listen to how a verse resonates within them. By the way, he called this morning; he spotted the first whales of the season in Gansbaai."

André pops up. "Enough with you two acting like snotty intellectuals. Let's go whale watching, instead. We've been toiling away like crazy these last weeks. We surely deserve a day off."

"That's fine with me," Cyril says grinning at her brother across the table.

The two men glance at Zoe at once.

"I'd rather stay home," she says too quickly. "I still have to write my report for Kuyper."

"Come on Zoe, it has been ages since we opened the whale season. I remember dad taking us there on a chilly day, picnicking on the beach, the wind feeling like a whetted knife."

She senses the story is being retold not for her sake but for Cyril's and dismisses it with an impatient gesture. *No need to share* with him *intimate moments of family life*. She goes back to her newspaper without saying a word.

"*Ousus* ..." André whispers close to her ear passing his fingers across the reddish pruning of her hair, as if to brush away her unruliness.

They probably think she's a spoilsport. How is it that some people can tackle life with such indomitable zest, living it down to the core, giving no chance for future regrets? Is one born with it or can it be acquired? Perhaps there are ways to be initiated into such a state. But she is going off track. The issue now is: Can she help André revive a beautiful memory?

"At what time were you thinking of leaving?"

"Now," André says, beaming. "Before you change your mind."

"I'll ask Georgina to help me prepare some sandwiches for our *padkos*."

❁❁❁

"I called Kurt," Cyril says as he gets into the car. "He'll meet us at the pier."

She should have expected this. Who knows, perhaps she even secretly hoped for it, despite her resolution never to see the thief of stories again.

"You two grew up together?" Zoe asks after a while as André drives them out of Franschhoek.

"Not really. He's ten years older than me. When I was a child, he was already a young man busy with his craft. We got to know each other better only later in life, after his release, when we were both living out of the country. I was eighteen when he was arrested. That day, I swore to myself I'd do everything to leave South Africa."

Zoe sticks one arm out of the window, feeling the breeze, trying to hide her impatience. She longs to know more about the man behind the writer.

"What was his father like?" she asks turning towards Cyril, who is sitting in the back seat.

"Afrikaner to the bone—very strict, very religious," Cyril says. "A brilliant magistrate. He could have easily become a judge at the Supreme Court. But when his son was sentenced to nine years' imprisonment his professional fortunes faded away."

"Kurt was in Pollsmore, wasn't he?" she asks again.

"*Ja.* His father knew the hell he would go through in there. He personally wrote to the President asking for a pardon. The request was rejected. Kurt got only two years off for good behaviour."

"What was he charged with exactly?" she asks.

"High treason. Subversive action against the state. He returned to South Africa from his self-imposed exile in France to re-establish a series of clandestine contacts within the ANC. They caught him four days after his arrival. Someone, probably from his close circle of comrades, betrayed him. He's adamant about that."

"Willem was at his wit's end when he found out that Van der Merwe had been invited to the reception," André says interrupting the barrage of her questioning. "I'd say he took it even worse than the news of Cyril's partnership."

"For Willem and his ilk, those like Kurt are the real traitors," Cyril says drily.

"Listen, I have no love for that kind of people, but put yourself in their shoes," André says glancing at him through the rear-mirror. "The genuine interpreter of the Boer's soul turns into a militant who attacks the political foundations of Afrikanerdom and incites resistance against apartheid. And he does so by shredding the *volk*'s mythology to pieces. Wouldn't you feel stabbed in the back?"

"No doubt," Cyril says, "despite my intrinsic difficulty in putting myself in Boer's shoes."

"Did he do all this from within South Africa?" Zoe asks, flaunting her brother's tacit call to self-restraint—or at least that's how she interpreted his interjections.

"*Nee.* At that point he'd already chosen to live in voluntary exile in Europe," Cyril says. "Here in South Africa censors kept themselves busy. You certainly wouldn't read about his tirades in the local newspapers."

"I have read some of them recently," André says.

"Did you?"

He chuckles, tapping gently on her thigh: "I'm not that dumb."

"Anyway, to him we Afrikaners are a nation of bastards, the offspring of the Dutch settlers interbreeding with their Khoikhoi, Malay and Malagasy slaves."

"Well, there's some historical truth in it, but that's quite a sweeping generalization."

André sneers lightly as he negotiates a bend on the narrow road: "Here is the voice from the academic pulpit."

"For the record, Kurt goes much further than that. It's expressly to cover up the most ambiguous traces of our genetic indignity that our *volk* resorted to a warped sense of racial purity. That's what he says."

"He speaks of collective self-delusion," Cyril says. "Unsure about its place and identity, a whole nation was made to believe that ethnic pride and culture could only descend from race."

"Whichever way you look at it, it was sheer madness," André says. "Mass mental perversion."

Zoe keeps quiet. She has never heard André talk so bluntly about their Afrikaner identity. That resentment in his voice is new to her. Perhaps he got caught up in the heat of the conversation. Or it may just be a considered pose for the benefit of the new black associate.

She decides not to read too much into it. Instead, she looks out of the window waiting for the blue line of the ocean to appear in the distance.

One and half hours later, they enter Gansbaai. From the car Zoe watches life amiably go by in this once small fishing village turned into holiday resort. Past are the days when white hunters lurked along this coastline waiting for the humpback and southern right whales to leave the feeding grounds off Antarctica, drawn by the call of the mating season.

They have parked the car and walked across the beach, to the pier. From there, the view stretches over a sequence of small coves and tranquil bays protected by cliffs abruptly dropping into the ocean. Zoe breathes in, filling her lungs with the salty air. It's a bright late autumn day, although its warmth is nullified by the brisk gusts of the south-western. She shivers in her jacket as she watches the ocean ripple and dance with light, the deep blue water turning green as it rolls against the cliff. It will be more difficult to spot whales in a sea so dishevelled.

"Too late, they're gone."

None of them has heard him arrive. Kurt greets Zoe with a wide smile before patting Cyril and André on the shoulder.

"Let's try the acoustic room and see if they're still around," he says tossing his jacket over a shoulder. He looks more at ease in his navy-blue pullover and canvas trousers than in his tuxedo.

"The acoustic room?" André asks.

"Yes, they opened it a couple of years ago to study whale sounds."

A few minutes later, they descend into an underwater chamber lying at the sea bottom, ten metres below the surface. Across the glass walls the seaweed dance gently in the current as a cacophony of wails, moans and shrieks starts enveloping the space.

"They're transmitted via a microphone applied to an offshore buoy," Kurt says.

The whales' vocalizations echo from wall to wall, filling the room with mysterious laments.

"Creepy," André murmurs.

"Whales emit sound to communicate and to echolocate," Kurt explains for his guests' sake. "When they dive, they receive and interpret the resulting echo as it is being reflected by the obstacles met on their way."

"In other words, they create acoustic images of their surroundings," Zoe says.

"Correct. They *see* by *hearing*."

"Nice way to put it," Cyril says.

Zoe listens more intently to the whales' eerie cries soundscaping an invisible territory, marking their wandering in the deserts of the deep. Through the glass wall she peers once more into that subaqueous world of vibrating solitudes, then follows the others toward the exit.

— 25 —

A DINNER INVITATION

THEY WALK ON the damp sand close to the shoreline marked by the lines of bygone tides.

They don't get to see any whales, but the fresh open air and the ocean's swell are just as good.

Later in the afternoon, Kurt invites them over. "I'll make dinner," he says. "Something simple, on the spot."

"No need to make up for having dragged us here for nothing," Cyril says to tease him.

On the way, Kurt stops at a grocery store to buy fresh produce. Standing on the pavement a few metres away from the outdoor stands Zoe watches as he picks veggies and exchanges a few jokes with the shop owner. He seems to bask in the ordinariness of simple gestures and easy talk. Back to basics. Is this what a life of dissidence, exile and imprisonment teaches you? Perhaps, this is *his* own way to make up for the prolonged loss of normalcy. Something happens to the brain. Now she can tell. After six months of self-confinement in a wasteland, even the simple furniture arrangement in her bedroom seems cluttered.

How does *he* see the world after seven years of forced captivity in a cell?

❁❁❁

Kurt's house, a simple bunker-like structure made of wood and stone, stands perched on a cliff between Gansbaai and Hermanus. The balcony protrudes from the building as if it were suspended in mid-air, between sea and sky.

"Well, that's what you'd call a view over infinity," André says leaning his arms on the rail at the edge of the terrace. "It's easy to become a lone wolf sitting up here with a Scotch, a good book, a little music in the background."

The sun, in the far west, is already an orange disk dipping in slow motion.

"I can't picture you in this role, André," Cyril says with a laugh.

"Neither can I," Zoe says.

But, then, why not? People change all the time, even when they think they don't.

"Anything to drink? Scotch on the rocks?" Kurt asks.

"I'm all for it," André says.

The wind has subsided. Cyril and her brother drop into the wicker chairs on the balcony and start chatting in low voices.

Kurt moves to the kitchen to prepare their drinks.

As she looks around, Zoe notices another window-door, slightly ajar, leading into a studio. She peers inside. Three of the walls are covered with books; in a corner facing the window is a sturdy desk of what looks like reclaimed wood; a computer and a stack of black leather notebooks are the only objects on it. She enters, walks over to the closest shelf and runs a finger over the spines of the books:

they're arranged in alphabetical order. She pauses at the V and reads the titles of his works.

"Here, Zoe," Kurt says, handing her a tumbler. She jumps slightly: He has come from behind, catching her by surprise.

"I'm sorry, I hope I'm not intruding."

"Not to worry," he says perching himself on a stool by the window: "A fossil hunter can't help being snoopy."

"I guess so," she says, listening to the ice tinkle against her glass. "Most of the time with few rewards, though. I mean, Mary Leakey found her first hominid footprints after she had wandered in the desert like a mad woman for thirty years."

He seems to wait for more. She can't suppress a smile.

"Is something funny?"

"I'm sorry. With your high-neck fisherman's sweater, whiskey in hand and unshaven stubble you look like a real writer. I mean, the way anyone would imagine, say, Hemingway in his study."

"Putting on weight, with greying hair and ready to shoot himself in the head. Too much like the old man, right?"

"I see you have most of his books."

"We never stop imitating our models, for better or for worse."

Out there, the sky has suddenly turned blood red. Below them, the Atlantic waves keep beating on the shore with dogged insistence.

As she turns again toward the shelf, Zoe makes eye contact with a young woman framed within a picture. She is of unusual beauty, with shiny black hair wrapping her shoulders like a silk shawl, slightly almond-shaped eyes and the golden-brown skin of the Cape Coloured.

Kurt stands up rather abruptly.

"You're going to miss the sunset," he says laying a hand on her hip, leading her gently through the window doors onto the terrace.

They reach the others in time to pick up what Cyril is saying: "He built this house with his own hands, soon after he came back to South Africa three years ago."

Zoe looks sideways to check Kurt's reaction, but he seems lost in his thoughts, perhaps in his memories. He keeps his eyes not on the fireball in the sky but down, at the relentless surf under their feet. Once again, he has retreated behind a curtain of cold detachment. Even his dwelling, so apparently open to the sun and the sea breeze, is standing within invisible walls – the ones he has erected between himself and the rest of the world.

Darkness is setting over the bay as they finish their drinks and follow Kurt into the kitchen, a large room with well-scrubbed pots and pans hanging by nails over the stove. Their host moves at ease in this space, with the dexterity of a man used to living alone. Zoe watches him as he chops onions, stir-fries veggies, cooks the pasta. For a moment, through these simple gestures, Dario's image superimposes itself on Kurt's, as if her dead lover had come to reclaim her.

"Italians devote a great deal of time and manic attention to food preparation," she blurts out in the surge of emotion. Only to regret it immediately.

André glances at her, puzzled.

"Indeed," Kurt says, unaware of the reasons for her verbal outburst. Then he adds, winking at Cyril: "I should've prepared a *potjiekos* instead."

"Do you honestly like that stuff?" Zoe asks glancing at their new director.

"He's teasing me," Cyril says, while he helps André set the table. "Our man of letters here is among those who decided to reclaim—in spite of it all—the dignity of the Afrikaner culture and language."

"And would you do it by submitting us all to Boer gastronomy?" she asks in a half-joking tone watching Kurt while he dishes up the pasta.

"Actually, as a social experiment I find it rather tasteful," he says passing the plates around.

Zoe falls quiet, not grasping the full meaning of his remark.

"It's not culinary art we're talking about here, *ousus*," André says coming to her aid. "It's about South Africa's future. While you were away, the concept of the *potjiekos* has been gaining traction among certain quarters of the Afrikaner intelligentsia."

"I see," she says.

"You're not great at cooking, admit it, Zoe," her brother says, keeping a playful tone. "But you know how to make *potjiekos*, right? You add layers of meat upon layers of vegetables and then let the whole thing simmer for hours. In this way, each layer flavours the others without losing its distinct taste." He pauses to see if she's following him; then says: "You never stir the *potjiekos*. If you mix its layers, all you get is an unpalatable meatloaf."

Zoe shakes her head, incredulous. Then, adjusting the plate in front of her, she asks, a bit too coldly: "So, by comparison, the American melting pot *is* the unpalatable meatloaf. Right?"

Her brother turns to Kurt, expecting him to answer. Their host takes a long sip from his glass of wine before answering.

"Listen, it's obvious that the different cultures of this country can no longer be separated from each other. Just like, once put to cook together in the *potjie* the meat layers can no longer be separated from the vegetable ones."

Kurt pauses to pour wine into her glass. "This doesn't necessarily mean you've to make a stew of them. Otherwise what you get is a vapid Rainbow Nation where all the ingredients blend and taste similar."

"A self-imposed apartheid without the police regime. Is this your 'new' recipe for this country?" Zoe asks looking at the three men in dismay.

"I wouldn't put it that way," Cyril says. "Kurt is right, diversity is healthy. We can accept each other and be together without giving up our differences. It's useless—even foolish—to reduce us to a common denominator."

"It might prove the only clever way out," she says, picking at her plate without much conviction.

"Why not look at Canada and Australia, instead?" her brother asks. "Their multicultural model seems to work."

"So far," Kurt says, smiling appreciatively at André. He has already emptied his plate and is ready for seconds. "In any case, theirs is a different history. We've got to find our own way."

"Don't get me wrong, Zoe. I'm all for cultural *métissage*, genetic mixing. Isn't this the way we evolved?" He briefly smiles at her before going on with his reasoning. "But these must be natural processes. You can't socially engineer hybridization nor integration. Just like you can't impose apartheid. The Rainbow Nation is an appealing brand name for a torn nation trying to heal itself, but it's a simplistic concept. Even trivial, I'd say, especially after what we've been through."

"What's the alternative, though?" she asks.

"The tribes of this country—the white, the black, the coloured—share a long history. Sure, a bloody and violent one. But we've been together for hundreds of years now. And, by the way, this is what sets us apart from Canada and Australia," Kurt says turning toward André. "This common lived history should be the foundation of our new country."

André nods. "Not a *fake* shared identity, but a mutual respect of our diversity."

In the silence that follows, everyone seems to be absorbed in their thoughts.

Her brother's remark brings Zoe back to one late-night conversation she had with Dario. His words still echo loud and clear: "*I'm anything but a racist, you know that. But let's be honest, Zoe. After a day of high exposure to multicultural interactions, if I want to relax I seek my people. I mean, those with whom I can speak freely, in my mother tongue; with whom, if I feel like it, I may even make an inappropriate joke without risking someone takes offence or without being accused of racism, classism, cynicism, or who knows what other -ism. This is a universal thing, a very human trait. And it happens to everyone across all cultures and continents.*"

Her brother breaks the silence, picking up the thread of the conversation. "So Kurt, you're willing to give the Afrikaner another chance in this land?"

"It all depends on how much longer we need to wallow in our Boer shame, using it as an alibi for inaction," their host replies looking sternly beyond the table, across the window, out at the black sea. "As a country, we can't collectively re-enter history from the front door if we still lack the main ingredient: self-respect."

"But we did evil. Who will take responsibility for that?" André asks.

"Group blame is a mistake, from whatever side of the fence you look at it," Kurt says, reaching for the cheese platter. "It all starts and ends with *the individual*. This we should remember."

"With due repentance, fathers and children are then acquitted of all charges," Cyril says with a hint of sarcasm, lifting his glass of Merlot to study its colour up to the light.

"With individual punishment *and* due collective reparation. Let's stick to the secular. Retribution, repentance, atonement are words that belong to another realm of judgment.

Zoe looks at Kurt's hands holding the cup of wine: *like a priest presiding at the celebration of the Eucharist.*

"I see where you're coming from," André says, playing with a cashew nut between his fingers. "As an individual, you've already paid your share. You rebelled against the fathers, the uncles, the brothers, and bore the consequences. But those of us who were tacitly complicit, who haven't fought, died or left this country when it was time to do so, how should we be feeling now?"

"Let everyone come to terms with oneself," Kurt says in a firm voice, knife still in hand for having just sliced more bread. He pauses, puts the knife down and adds: "Each one of us should establish what he or she gave to or took away from this country, do the sums and then take action."

He gazes at his interlocutors, checking their reaction, then says: "What I'm trying to say is that, until we stick to this ethnic *curse*, until we accept to be branded as 'dirty Afrikaners' by the world, we won't be free to think—and act—in new ways, nor feel responsible for one another."

Zoe notices that their host has uttered the word *vloek* (curse) not in Afrikaans, the language in which they are conversing, but in English, as if to emphasize its intolerable impact.

"One first step towards this 'freedom' might be to stop thinking of ourselves as Europeans," Kurt says. "We're Africans, now."

She sits back, unable to contain a surge of annoyance in her tone of voice. "To become *truly* African we have to reject Europe as such. Is this what you're telling us?"

"I don't disown our European blood. But we must accept our forebears were expelled from that world, for economic, religious or political reasons. Very few made for the Cape just for the sheer thrill of adventure. If anything, we can now claim the right to be a separate people."

"Good point," André says. "Americans don't think of themselves as former Brits. My question then is: How can we claim to be African if, just to give a trivial example, at rugby matches we can sing only the 'Die Stem' bit of the anthem because we didn't even care to learn the 'Nkosi Sikelel' iAfrika' part?"

"We'll get there," Kurt replies. "Once we convince ourselves this is the way forward, which is also what tells us apart from the old world."

"Meaning?"

"Blinded by their affluence and self-righteousness, Europeans don't realize they're drifting toward another form of socio-ethnic apartheid—less visible, perhaps, but not less insidious." Once again Kurt stops and looks around the table at his guests. She, like the others, just sits staring at him, waiting for him to tell them more. "They are inadvertently building their own *laager*. It's a regression, a replication of past oversights, and certainly not the way to go. We know it because we've already been there and borne its dire consequences. Your fortress becomes a prison once you have swarms of desperate people pressing at the gate."

They all keep quiet for a while, picking at the grapes and nuts from the cheese board, then looking at the wine in their glasses.

"The interesting part of our writer's theory," Cyril says, breaking the silence, "is for all this process of Africanization of the *volk* to happen, Afrikaners still need to put up a fight."

The mockery in their partner's tone is subtle but eloquent.

"What does *that* mean?" Zoe asks turning toward Kurt.

"Being white and Afrikaner in the new South Africa means having the wrong skin colour," he replies, ignoring the sarcasm in Cyril's remark. "Culturally, linguistically, now we are a minority under threat of extinction. That's what drew me back."

"How lucky I am to be black these days ..." Cyril says, raising his glass to toast the company. Zoe realizes their partner is trying to lighten the tone, even though his friend's words are not easy to digest.

"I guess you're one of those writers who write best from a position," she says, the words falling off her somewhat dryly.

"Not necessarily," Kurt replies.

"Anyway, I'd think twice before disavowing your European heritage," Cyril says. "For me, it's in Europe, among more or less enlightened white people, that I found my dignity. Not in the States—still too racist, although I'm greatly indebted to that country."

Kurt nods meekly to his friend, as if realizing he's gone too far. Then he looks up from his cup of wine and searches Zoe's eyes. She can't be sure, but has the impression he's made an effort to come out of his solitary confinement. By opening a chink in his protective wall he's tried to reveal a part of himself. To her.

❁❁❁

When the time comes to take their leave, André and Cyril shake hands with their host and quickly disappear along the narrow path into the night, heading for the car.

Zoe is left alone with Kurt in the halo of light from the back porch. He turns slowly toward her.

"I'm told you'll be leaving soon for your desert."

She nods.

"And you won't come back until you've found what you are looking for."

How is she to interpret his words: as a question, a confirmation, an order?

"Another six months in the dust," she says, averting her eyes.

He senses her turmoil and gently touches her lips with the thumb of his left hand.

"But you know you'll come back to the ocean."

Zoe keeps her eyelids lowered. Her chin, however, is now facing up, towards him. He draws her to him and kisses her, ever so lightly. It's an instant of bliss. Yet, she rapidly collects herself and withdraws, frightened by her sudden weakness. He pauses, on his face a sudden expression of dismay—then, of regret.

Zoe swivels and runs away, leaving him there in the doorway, without even a good-bye. She climbs into the car, her heart still pounding wildly.

❁❁❁

On the day of her departure, Zoe receives a small parcel. "A man left it here this morning. Didn't say a word," Georgina says. She turns it over in her hands: no sender. Before opening it, Zoe tries to guess its contents. It might be a book. Indeed: It's a copy of *The Secret Sharer and Other Stories* by Joseph Conrad, accompanied by a short letter written in the thick ink of a fountain pen and nervous, unconventional handwriting.

Zoe,

I thought I was well past the age when one gets carried away, acts on an impulse, follows the instinct of the moment. Evidently, I was wrong.

I hope you will allow me to make amends in due course.

In the desert, in prison or out at sea, Conrad can be a good companion. I found in his pages a way to exorcise, at least in part, the darkest moments of my life.

May your search in the wilderness be rewarding.

Kurt

She reads the letter again, slowly absorbing it. Then takes the book and strokes the cover, thinking of Kurt's hands, which she has so rudely stopped. She wishes she could follow him in his world of well-chosen words. Instead, she folds his letter and hides it inside the book.

She leaves without replying.

— 26 —

NIGHT OF THE TRANCE

FOR ANOTHER FIVE months Zoe and her team keep digging and sweating.

Unsuccessfully.

"We need a change," she tells Moses one evening opening Dario's map. Eight weeks have passed since the men came back from their second break. She senses the fragile harmony of the camp might not survive another month of unfruitful efforts.

"Here," she says putting her finger on the fourth and last red circle drawn by Dario. It marks the location of a group of modest rocky outcrops known as the Ahaberge —the Aha Hills. They protrude from the flat belly of the plain as rough, pointy breasts.

"The Bushmen keep away from those *koppies*," Sam says with his usual streak of mocking unconcern, looking in the direction of the hills, which stand out from the thorny scrub some thirty kilometres to the north-east. "They claim the spirits of the dead hover over the place. Someone even swears having seen horses there, running wild, mounted by screaming baboons."

She squints suspiciously. He smiles candidly as he stretches back, hands locked behind his head, elbows out.

"Baboons?" Wally asks.

"*Ja*, the San believe they're the souls of those who, in the hour of death, haven't realized they're dead."

Wally keeps his eyes low; Lionel, Shadrack and Steve shuffle their boots in the sand with apparent uneasiness. Not even Moses seems enthusiastic about Zoe's idea.

She gives Sam a cross look, struggling to control her anger. *She* will not tolerate having her expedition jeopardized by an impertinent *dagga* addict set on poking fun at his mates. She has kept the Aha Hills as the final stage of her expedition and won't back down now.

She turns to Moses and tries to give a forceful tone to her voice: "Professor Oldani did circle this spot. We will give it a try." Then looking sternly in Sam's eyes: "At least we'll leave the flatland—300 metres up."

❁❁❁

The day before they head for the hills, Koma walks up to her.

"Tonight, we'll talk to your shadow."

Zoe keeps quiet, looking out at the dreary stretch of dust and grass.

She has pushed herself too far. Half a century ago Great Aunt Adèle entered a *sangoma's* hut seeking a "cure" that would break her free. To no avail. Perhaps there are doors that shouldn't be opened, or lead nowhere. Who can tell?

"Are you sure?" she asks.

The old man looks straight at her, as if he were assessing her, then says: "The wind doesn't respect words lightly said. Too quickly they fly away."

A half-smile finds its way to her lips. *Kurt would like the way the old man speaks.*

She takes a deep breath: "This is it, then."

"Come when you hear the women singing."

That's all, no other instructions.

❁❁❁

Just before sunset the wind begins to blow across the plain, carrying its breath through the camel thorn, swaying the collective nests of the sociable weaver-birds. It bursts in gusts, full of the scents of the veld. The forces of nature have been mustered. The scene is set.

At dinner, Zoe sits aside, with no desire to talk. Later on, while she's having her rooibos, Sam approaches her. She smells the acrid smoke of the *dagga* imprisoned in his wool cap.

"Koma told me you'll be entering the trance circle tonight."

"Did he?" she says drily, still angry at him.

"Perhaps he thought you might need a chaperone," he says.

"I see."

"You look worried, *Mejuffrou.*"

She feels her lips quivering, like those of a child about to cry. Sam looks away and gives her time to gather herself.

She takes a sip from her tin cup, still undecided. Then, in a low voice: "It feels strange, even a bit scary, I must say."

"If you're lucky, it's gonna get a hold on you."

"And then what happens?

"Nothing. Just pure bliss. That's when the healing starts."

"How will I know?"

"No need to know, you'll feel it."

She keeps quiet.

"I can come with you if you wish. I got their permission."

"Would you?"

"It'd be an honour."

A few minutes later, darkness drops like a heavy curtain on the Kalahari. Then, something unusual happens. Although the rainy season is still far away, flares of electrical discharge pierce the night cover, creating fluorescent patterns over the horizon. After the lightning comes the thunder, rolling boulders along the prairie sky.

From the *kraal* a litany of acute feminine voices rises into the blackness.

"It's time," Sam says.

She picks up the torch and follows Sam along the path to the village. She sticks to the narrow cone of light in front of her, her eyes fixed on the ground, her mind suddenly gone blank.

When they reach the women chanting around the campfire, Sam motions for her to sit on the sidelines, just outside the circle. Some of the women dance with their babies tied in a blanket on their backs, others stand crouched on the ground, weaving their voices together into an elementary polyphony punctuated by the obsessive rhythm of their hand-clapping. The lightning keeps whizzing across the black dome over their heads, revealing in flashes the huts, the bare breasts, the children's sleepy eyes.

Zoe takes a peek at Sam out of the corner of her eye. He has taken off the wool cap and the long, braided Rasta hair now tumbles over his shoulders and face. He keeps his eyes closed, waiting. The night has turned into a cold hand; Zoe feels its fingers pierce her light coat and cling to her body.

Then, all of a sudden, Koma and the village shaman, Khao, come out of the night, making their way into the circle of firelight. They advance in small steps, singing with husky voices, stomping their feet on the ground. They're naked but for a leather loincloth tied at the waist. They keep dancing around the fire, leaning forward on their sticks. marking the tempo with their rattles, made of insect cocoons filled with ostrich egg-shell splinters. The singing intensifies in pitch, the beat of the rattle drumming accelerates.

Khao lets out a high-pitched howl. He starts shaking and swaying, then staggers out of the circle of light.

"He's in a trance, now," Sam tells Zoe, pointing with a tiny head nod at the old shaman.

Clinging to her scientist's mind, Zoe takes a mental note: Khao has reached his trance state through sheer mind power, apparently without ingesting or smoking any psychogenic substances.

"What about Koma?"

"He's only in a semi-trance. He's in attendance, you see?"

Zoe watches the old shaman from Schmidtsdrift hold his companion, direct him with his singing and the relentless beat of the rattles.

The two men step back into the circle. Then, still singing, Khao leans over one of the women, lays one hand on her chest and one on her back. He flutters his hands as if they were little wings. All along he keeps moaning, grunting, mumbling words Zoe can't understand.

"He's talking to the spirits," Sam explains, "chasing the demons away. Drawing the sickness out through his arms—taking it into himself."

The old shaman goes on with his healing work through gasps and piercing cries, laying his trembling hands on every person in the circle and then throwing up his arms, as if he could really cast the sickness out, hurl it into the black sky. He often rushes to the fire, teetering dangerously over it; Koma is always there to hold him, preventing him from falling into it.

"When they're in that state they feel their body as cold as frost at dawn," Sam says. "They try to warm it up as best as they can."

The singing, the clapping, the stomping never cease, never lose their intensity and rhythmic precision.

Khao has almost completed the circle of healing when Koma motions for Zoe to follow him.

As she gets up, Sam whispers: "Don't fight it."

Koma leads her into the circle and has her sit down among the women, then takes Khao by the shoulders and gently directs him towards her. She is stunned by fright, feels gooseflesh crawl on her skin. At the same time, she's drawn to the obsessive rhythm of the rattles, the mysterious breath coming from the desert, the shrill voices of the singing women, and by this old naked man now in front of her, lost in his trance—so far away, unreachable.

Zoe makes an effort to calm down, breathing deeply. She crosses her legs, rests the palms of her hands on her knees, closes her eyes and tries to focus on the nothingness. She wants to get rid of every thought, every sparkle of her rational mind. She visualizes herself stripped of her scientist's garb, willing to offer herself in her most primitive, human form.

The firelight dances on her eyelids, she hears Khao's laboured breathing come closer and then feels his quivering hands first on her neck and then on her chest—they are pure energy. She keeps her eyes closed, feeling there's no need to open them: She can see him without looking at him. For an instant, all barriers—between her, Sam, the San people, her language, their language, her skin, their skin—crumble.

Khao hisses, moans and then, after what seems to her a long spell of silence, lets out a piercing scream. He withdraws his hands. The women's singing stops. The ratt-atatta-ta of the rattles against the men's calves fades away. Only the crackling of the campfire keeps going.

Zoe stops breathing, her heart misses a beat, or so she feels. She doesn't want to open her eyes, not knowing what to expect. The silence is short lived. The ratt-at-at-ta-ta starts again, along with the hand clapping and the women's singing.

With her eyes still firmly shut, Zoe feels Khao's hands on her chest again.

And here again comes this galvanizing feeling of being inside a limitless womb of light, safe and warm. She loses track of time, because time has ceased to exist. She is living through her skin pores, absorbing all this light. She is blind, yet she can see everything, *feel* everything.

It is pure, emotional joy.

Three times the shaman puts his hands on her; each time Zoe feels these quivering hands don't belong to him, an old shrivelled old man, but to a luminous girl. And *this girl* keeps wailing, whining, sending her high-pitched shrieks through the sky.

Until, all of a sudden, the night falls silent again. Reluctantly, she opens her eyes, as the women and children casually shuffle back to their huts. It's Koma who, finally, takes her by the arm and helps her up.

"*Loop*. Go now." That's all he says.

❁❁❁

As she and Sam head off to the camp in the dark, leaving behind them the halo of the campfire, Zoe sees Khao's body lying apparently lifeless on the ground. Two women are rubbing his chest, another is passing hot coals over his body. She watches worriedly, as a trickle of blood flows from the shaman's nostrils.

"It's not your fault, *Mejuffrou*. It's often the case," Sam says following her gaze. "It'll take him a few hours to recover."

Zoe has already slipped back into her scientist mode. She kneels by Khao's inert body and places two fingers on his wrist looking for a pulse. The heart rate is dangerously slow, like that of a comatose person. This man knows the secret to kiss death on her lips and withdraw just before she can entice him forever.

❁❁❁

Back at the camp, Zoe lies awake in her cot for a long time, her eyes open onto the slate of a starless sky. She thinks of Khao. The old shaman has offered her something inexplicable. Sam is right: There are no words for it. She has been part of a ritual as old as the desert. A "living fossil" has showed her the true meaning of joy—pure, ecstatic, unselfish joy. But it all might be an illusion, a short-lived entrainment into a hypnotic state. It all might be the workings of a mind —*her* mind—lost at sea, desperately seeking its bearings.

After all, she is nothing but a poor human being biting into the thorns of existence.

❁❁❁

The next morning, Zoe struggles to get up. The sun hasn't risen yet, but the men in the camp are already up and about. The smell of coffee reaches her and pushes her out of her sleeping bag. Once dressed, she joins her crew for breakfast. Then looks for Koma, sitting outside his hut. A glance at his inscrutable face is enough to tell her that he won't talk to her today; he won't reveal whether her shadows have been vanquished. His words will come at the right time.

— 27 —
SORROW

AUNT CLAIRE'S IS the story Zoe remembers best. Yet, she now wants to revisit it through her words, written in elegant but resolute handwriting. She's seeking consolation in the inked voice of someone who already travelled along the same barren road. Or, perhaps, she needs a tragic story to indulge in self-commiseration, as her aunts did in the past.

It's a moonless night in the bush. Zoe withdraws into her tent carrying the gas lamp and pulls out Aunt Claire's diary from the satchel.

She doesn't open the pages at random. She knows what she is looking for.

Franschhoek, April 14, 1966

Today I saw Gerard again, by pure accident. He took me off guard. I did some errands in Cape Town and, before coming home, I stopped for a cup of tea in Long Street. The waitress had just laid the pot on my table when I saw him. He stood in front of me, hunched in his baggy jacket, the collar of his white shirt stained and unbuttoned. Two years had passed since the day I had run away from him, in that cold dawn. He looked dismal, worn down, his face gaunt, his eyes devoured by an inner fever. Still beautiful though—like a fallen angel. I sat there, speechless.

His hands were smeared with colour, as they were on that night when they explored my body. It was pure madness—risking his life for one breath of love! I had rushed out of his studio in panic. Then, back in my room, I had looked in the mirror and followed with my thumb the strokes of Prussian blue on my breasts and the Sienna fingermarks running deep inside my thighs. He had left his signature on my body.

Finally, he broke the silence. He said he had waited for me, night after night, working like a madman, filling canvas upon canvas with my absence. I saw his jaw muscle tighten, a bitter grimace suddenly marred his face. His torment was almost palpable. "How ironic," he said, shaking his head. "In London, they like my desperado paintings." As he spoke I couldn't take my eyes off his arms, dangling loosely at his side. All of a sudden he had become a rich man, he told me, and then added: "Like your father would have liked, I suppose." That bit crushed me. His stare was as hard as stone. I found it difficult to breathe.

"Do you have someone else, Claire?" he asked, burning his eyes into mine. I tried to speak, but I couldn't utter a word. I felt like I had just bitten into a mouthful of sand. My lips stuck together.

"Do you have someone else?" he asked again.

I gestured for him to sit at the table, but he stood there, his dark curls tumbling unkempt over his face. He kept squeezing his hands into fists.

All the feelings that for months I had stifled with great effort came back to me in a rush. I still loved him. Fiercely. I would have given anything to be his muse, his concubine, his slave. Instead, I could do nothing but drift away from him—a shadow without a master.

Finally, I managed to repeat what I had already promised him that night, that he would always be the only one: "That was our deal, Gerard." At this point, he opened his fists, stretched his long fingers and let out a resinous groan, like a tree burning from the inside. He drew a chair to my side, sat down and, with infinite tenderness, took my hand in his.

"Why don't you come back then? Where did I go wrong?"

I begged him not to torment himself. Again, I restated that the problem was not him, it was me.

"Why lie so shamelessly?" he cried, rising abruptly to his feet. I could feel the full tension of his body, a tightrope about to snap. He said that he felt my pleasure under his hands. That he knew how to recognize a woman in love. That yes, he had had many lovers, but it was me he wanted for life. That, without me, he was lost.

He was about to break. And I with him. He retook his seat.

Trying to hide my pain, I mentioned his talent: "You said it yourself: It's my absence that makes you paint the way you do ..."

He let a thick silence fall upon us.

I looked at my dark brew. When I raised my eyes again to meet his, I cringed. In them, I could only read what he had once called "the yellowness of hatred, the acridity of contempt." He had used that same colour and that same unforgiving stare for the portrait of a man betrayed by his companions. Now he was pasting it onto himself. Meant for me.

He stood up and, before taking his leave, he stabbed me with these words: "Claire Du Plessis, behind your soft lips there hides a ruthless woman. Your family name has made you haughty and contemptuous. I despise you, even though I can't stop loving you."

After he left, I kept looking at my hands, clasping the saucer. How long I sat there, staring at the rotten fabric of my existence, I don't know. I barely registered when it got dark and they turned on the lights in the café. Finally, the waitress came up to my table: "We're about to close." I paid and went out into the dusk.

The next entry in Aunt Claire's diary is dated four days later.

Franschhoek, April 20, 1966

Gerard is dead. He killed himself. I found it out in the most brutal way, reading the evening newspaper: "Gerard Pienaar, the thirty-five-year-old artist from Cape Town who managed to break into the London art scene with his vibrant works, was found dead this morning in his studio by his cleaning lady, Mrs. Priscilla Arends. Forensic analysis determined that he committed suicide with a lethal dose of cyanide. No suicide note was found."

There follows an entire page to commemorate Gerard's figure as an artist that Aunt Claire must have copied from another newspaper. A subsequent note also seems to have been taken from a newspaper article:

> *"In his will, which the artist dictated to his executor just three days before his death, Gerard Pienaar left all his works to the South African National Gallery in Cape Town except for one picture titled 'Sorrow,' which at his explicit request is to be delivered to a woman whose identity must not be publicly disclosed."*

The diary ends on a last short note.

> *Franschhoek, 27 April 1966*
>
> *I didn't attend his memorial service, which was held privately by the family. Yesterday, at five in the afternoon, a mailman delivered my funeral gift. I'll never let anyone see this canvas. I will keep it rolled up in the trunk, and, when my time comes, I will make sure that it will be buried with me. I will live with the pain of his absence, as he lived with mine, albeit for a much shorter time.*

Zoe closes the diary and holds it between her hands, under the chin. She sits there, on a military cot, in the laden-grey light cone of a hand torch, listening to her thoughts.

She has become a prisoner of her family's plotline. Like her aunts, she has come to identify herself with a character in a pre-set script written by someone else. The sense of inevitability enveloping her life is becoming unbearable.

She feels trapped in a cage of predestination, with invisible bars and no rescue plan. She rushes out of the tent, gasping for air. The bush is dipped in black, shrouded in silence. The camp fire is dying down, no one tending its flame. She has never felt so utterly alone.

— 28 —

DISENCHANTMENT

"**There is no** permanent source of water in the vicinity. Animal life is scarce — just a few birds, the occasional insect. The stillness is near perfect, the silence arresting. The place eerie to the extreme." Zoe jotted down this note in her field journal the day they tackled the Aha Hills. A few weeks later, as a post scriptum to her regular entry, she added: "So far, no one has seen black baboons riding on horseback, or screaming obscenities to the big sky."

After two months spent exploring the area, the team's efforts are now concentrated in one place: a cave they have discovered at the foot of the hills. It's a relief for Zoe and her workers to enter this cool earth's womb while out there the land scorches in the fierce sun.

Past its spacious entrance, the cave makes an "S" bend before narrowing sharply downwards for about fifty metres. At the end of a black tunnel, slippery with rubble, there lies a small chamber lined with rounded rocks.

Zoe spends most of her time underground now, studying by torchlight the silent alphabet of rocks, sediments and remains of prehistoric animals relentlessly unearthed by the team. The cave must have sheltered generations of predators and — hopefully — humans.

Always by her side, Moses works fast and efficiently.

❁❁❁

The rainy season comes without them hardly taking notice.

"Down there you guys are missing a formidable show," Daniel tells Zoe one late afternoon as they both watch distant rumbling clouds challenge the inert high-pressure system. A few days later, the clouds are closer, bigger; they hover over the midday heat waves like giant cathedrals.

Then one afternoon, drawn by the sudden commotion coming from the entrance of the cave, she climbs out of her lair and finds herself in a crashing downpour. The rain pelts down impetuously, as if to establish its sudden, although ephemeral, supremacy on the parched land. The earth receives it like a courtesan would welcome in her bed the crusader just returned from the Holy Land: with docile, yet eager submission.

The men are all dancing around, shouting and singing. Zoe walks away from them and, raising her face upwards, lets the sky's tears rush over her. Her khaki shirt, now sodden, adheres to her body and she feels her nipples stiffen at the contact. With her eyes still closed, she imagines Dario's lips on hers. Then, all of the sudden, it's not him but Kurt she is trying to kiss.

❁❁❁

A few weeks later, Koma walks into the camp while Zoe is busy cleaning up oryx bones. The sun is already low in the sky.

"*Kom*, Zoe. To the waterhole. This is a good time."

A good time for what? For talking? For watching a sunset? For just being? She follows him, walking along the narrow path through the tall verdant grass. With the rains, what until not long ago looked like an inconspicuous salt pan now brims with water. An array of animals come here again to quench their thirst. She and Daniel have spotted impalas, warthogs, bat-eared foxes, hyenas. This time, the silence that envelops the place has a surreal edge.

Koma crouches on a small outcrop of flat rocks and Zoe squats by his side. As usual, behind a seemingly indolent attitude the old shaman conceals full mental vigilance. He misses nothing: the smells carried by the breeze, the warning signal given by a weaver bird, the faint track left by a honey badger. Suddenly, his whispering alert tears Zoe away from her thoughts.

"*Olifante.*"

She looks around but can't see nor hear any sign of them. They both sit motionless for a few more minutes, in a world gradually turning copper coloured. At last, she spots them: silent, dusty shadows moving slowly through the bushes, delicate in their heavy sway. Zoe counts at least seven female pachyderms, some of them with their calves holding on their tails or following behind. Before reaching the pan, the matriarch sniffs the air with her raised trunk; satisfied with her reconnaissance, she trots blithely towards the water followed by the rest of the herd.

Zoe takes her time to watch the scene, then turns to look at Koma. His gaze is fixed on the horizon, his expression unreadable. After a long while the old shaman speaks: "The shadow is still with you, *Mejuffrou*. We couldn't chase it away."

❁❁❁

That night, Zoe hands Sam two letters and a parcel to be delivered the following day to the post office in Tsumkwe. The first letter is addressed to Professor Kuyper and contains a detailed report on the latest excavation site, with the request to extend for at least another six months her research in the Kalahari. The second letter and the parcel are meant for Kurt.

Kurt,

Thank you for the book and the note with which you accompanied me into the desert. I never thanked you for that, fearing I might show any tender inclination towards you. I entrust you with the diaries of my aunts and the family's secret they contain. By reading them, you'll understand the reasons for my aloof silence.

Like all the Du Plessis who came before me, I too didn't want to believe, couldn't believe in the reality of a supernatural cause to our disgrace. Someone else paid for my skepticism. One year ago, my partner died in a hijacking. Yet another coincidence?

Evidently, we cannot escape the past.

You are a writer. Who knows, one day you might find a way to put to good use the story of the Du Plessis.

Zoe

That's all she can grant Kurt.

❁❁❁

Two weeks later, Daniel pays a visit to the camp bringing with him the mail, including two letters for Zoe. The first one is a telegram from Kuyper:

> *Granted three-month extension. Stop. Not more than that. Stop.* Homo sapiens' *footprints found in Langebaan. I advise to leave ASAP for the Cape. Stop.*

The second is a letter from Kurt, written in his nervous handwriting. Zoe retires to her tent to read it.

> *Zoe,*
>
> *The trust you have confided in me, together with your aunts' diaries, is a precious gift. Remarkably, your female ancestors were adept at storytelling. All of them. I felt with them when I read what they wrote as they choked back tears, remorse, anger. And I thought of you up there, trying to find a way out from a chain of deadly recurrences.*
>
> *By sending me these diaries, you have broken the conspiracy of silence.*
>
> *Ancestral heritage and modernity, religious superstition and scientific evidence have been at war for centuries. You are a woman of science, but for too long the Afrikaner blood flowing in your veins has been pressing against the temples and obscured your sight.*
>
> *Time to let go. Leave the past to whom it belongs: the dead. I will try to do the same.*
>
> *The memory of you is like water flowing softly through my fingers. Don't stop its course.*
>
> *Kurt*

She walks out of the tent. Still holding the letter in her hand, she turns her head up to the sun. The harsh mid-day light bites into her eyelids. Without mercy.

❁❁❁

Eight more weeks slip away, uneventful. Then, one afternoon in which Zoe stays behind to classify their recent findings, Moses comes back to the camp much earlier than expected. His eyes shine with satisfaction as he hands her what he's just discovered in the cave. It's an almond-shaped flint, symmetrically flaked on both faces, which gives it a cunning sharpness. Zoe touches the rudimentary stone object as if it were a precious jewel. Its features are the result of a Palaeolithic mind at work.

As for the type of *Homo* (*ergaster*? *habilis*? *erectus*? *sapiens*?), this is up to them to discover.

The dark cave where she has retreated for so long, keeping away from the outer world, has finally talked to her. Overwhelmed, she firmly embraces her crew leader, holding him to her chest, all the while whispering: "*Dankie, dankie, dankie.*"

Moses doesn't say a word, but his big and slightly puzzled smile talks for him. For over a year this man has tried to comply with her seemingly absurd needs and requests. Too many times has he seen her disappear into that cave as if it were a temple, a place of worship. Until a chipped stone, a small prehistoric hand axe, finally has brought her to herself.

— 29 —

THE MISSION

THE EXTRA THREE months granted by Kuyper are coming to an end with no other significant discoveries from the bowels of the Aha Hills. Still, she's not ready to quit. The cave has just shown them a glimpse of what it's jealously hiding. "It will open up again," she keeps telling Moses. "We can't give up now. Not so easily."

❁❁❁

One late afternoon, driving into the camp after yet another day spent in the cave, Zoe spots Daniel's Land Rover parked behind the kitchen tent. As she slows down, ready to stop, two other men wearing large-brimmed safari hats busy talking to Wally turn around and walk over to where the ranger is waiting for her.

"I brought you a couple of guests," Daniel says, rushing to open the door of her Land Rover without even waiting for the dust to clear. He has a sheepish look, like a child expecting to be reprimanded. She looks over his shoulder and meets her brother's and Cyril Kunene's grinning faces.

"What are you doing here?" she asks, without concealing her irritation.

"Here's your rescue team!" André cries half-heartedly, taken aback by her cold reception.

"Oh, so I'm the crazy woman lost in her desert who needs to be saved from herself?"

Zoe can feel her upper lip trembling, revealing—she is sure—her anguish and her anger, for she suddenly feels her world has been violated.

"I spoke with Kuyper. He was okay with us coming to visit you," her brother says, stammering, unsure of how to deal with this sister of his, so unexpectedly distant, lost in a dimension unknown to him. "And he gave me this. For you ..."

He reaches into his rucksack to pull out a manila envelope. Zoe opens it and finds a formal invitation to the 1997 International Conference on Paleoanthropology, to be held in one month's time in Zanzibar. She goes through it quickly and sees that she's scheduled to give the keynote speech. Title: "Southern Africa as the cradle of humankind: an alternative hypothesis."

"What nerve! He knew I wouldn't agree. It's way too early to make any such assumptions—at least publicly."

"Kuyper sounded quite positive about it," André says. "He stated that with Lady J and your recent finding up here you had enough to make a case."

"Then he needs a PR woman, not a scientist," she says. "How come you talked to *my* boss, if I may?"

"I called him to let him know I wished to visit you to discuss important family matters. That's all."

She lets out a sardonic chuckle.

"I thought you could show us the Kalahari and, in

return, we'd help you decamp," André says changing the subject and trying to ease his way out of the tense exchange.

"No objections to having you as my guests," Zoe says. "As for decamping, when the time comes I have my team and won't need any extra help."

André looks at his sister in puzzlement, ever more abashed by her off-putting reaction. He keeps quiet, though.

Zoe turns to Daniel and says: "Be so kind please to bring my guests back with you when you leave."

The bushranger nods, tipping his hat with his middle and index fingers and rushes to unload fresh produce from the Land Rover.

Zoe glances at Cyril, who all this time has kept himself to the sidelines.

Why is he here? This is family business.

Her brother doesn't seem to care. He charges again, his jaw visibly tense. "Is it true that you've been practically living inside the cave where you've been digging?"

"Who told you such nonsense?" she says.

She actually knows where this information comes from. During his last visit, Daniel showed a certain apprehension about the manic doggedness with which she was devoting herself to her underground excavations. She tries to meet his eye, but the ranger is already off, walking briskly toward the camp kitchen.

"Is it true or not?" André asks.

In the sudden quiet, there comes the faint noise of an engine hurtling across the scrub. Moses and the rest of the team will soon be back.

"The cave—my *lair*—is an hour's drive from here,"

Zoe finally says stretching her arm to grab the backpack from inside the jeep. "Tomorrow, right after breakfast, I'll take you there for a grand tour of the premises. And yes, I have slept there a couple of times, against Moses' best judgment."

Trying to ease the tension of her own making, she adds: "Dinner will be served soon. I'm sure Wally has cooked something special to welcome you."

André and Cyril look at each other without saying a word.

❁❁❁

That evening, after dinner, none of the workers stay behind for a smoke and a chat by the fire. They instead follow Sam and Daniel to the bushmen's village, from which come the sounds of singing and dancing.

They're alone now—Zoe, her brother and Cyril. No one seems eager to break the silence.

André lights one of his Gitanes and blows a long plume of smoke into the night. Then, keeping his eyes closed, he begins to speak: "For years you kept me unaware of your torments, *ousus*—you, the eldest daughter of our family ..."

She gasps. He knows! Her mind rushes to Kurt. Betrayed—she almost gags at that sudden, horrible feeling. But, anticipating her reaction, her brother makes a reassuring gesture, demanding not to be interrupted. "I haven't been honest with you either." Then, his eyes fixed on hers, he says: "There will be no descendants of the Du Plessis in our family." He pauses, draws from his cigarette again and throws the rest of it into the fire. "At least not from my side."

He pronounces the last words mechanically, dropping his arms to his sides, like a puppet whose strings had been suddenly cut. Then he turns slowly towards Cyril and smiles at him with sad sweetness. Who knows how many times before tonight André has repeated these words to himself—a solitary actor rehearsing his lines. She watches the thin web of wrinkles that has started to make its way across her brother's face. Only his eyes remain those of the child in the attic.

"We've been hiding our relationship and you know why, Zoe," Cyril says, coming into play under a new light.

The anger rapidly washes out of her system. The unexpected revelation of her plight takes a back seat now that she's confronted with *their* secret. It could have cost them dearly under apartheid's draconian laws against homosexual and interracial relationships.

Zoe watches the two men in front of her, their faces animated by the web of light and shadow cast by the flickering fire. They look so different from each other—one almost as pearly as the morning mist, the other carved in dark wood. Yet they both look at ease now that the weight of imposed silence and shame has been lifted. Perhaps this is what it means to be free, after all.

"You've left me speechless," she says, her elbows on her knees, her hands cupping her chin. "I look at the two of you and it's like I'm seeing you for the first time."

"Perhaps we belong to a new species, which still has to be studied," André says. "A species useless for reproductive purposes, I'm afraid."

She jumps up and goes to kneel behind her brother, putting her arms around his shoulders and pressing her chest against his back. André places his hands on hers, grateful for this gesture of recognition. They are close again, as close as ever possible.

"Let's talk about you, *ousus*," André says.

"Not tonight," she replies, suddenly stiffening.

He takes both her hands in his, passing a finger over the scratches, the bruises, the nails lined with dirt.

"Is the finding of a single flaked piece of flint enough for you to believe that down in that cave there could lie something relevant?" André asks.

"Sometimes a lot less suffices."

Zoe lies awake in her cot, under the pitch-black vault of the sky. Since she came into the bush she has never seen so many stars hanging up there. Thoughts pop in and out of her head—disorderedly, incongruously. Kurt broke her trust, burning her first steps out of the cage. André has finally someone by his side. While she is alone, again. She should drop all sense of responsibility, for once. Break the camp rules, renounce her self-inflicted discipline. Take a shower. Yes, a shower. A long one. One that can wash away the resentment, the rancid smell of self-pity.

When sleep comes, it comes to her with surprising swiftness, out of sheer exhaustion.

Early the next morning, Zoe walks out of the tent and, in the glimmering half-darkness that precedes dawn, makes out the silhouette of Cyril crouching by the fire. She walks slowly but resolutely to him and sits down by his side, her back straight, her neck aching from the tension.

"*Goeiemôre*, Zoe," Cyril says. "Just in time for a fresh brew."

She doesn't reply.

They drink from their cups in the silence only broken by the crackling of the fire and the soft singing of the weaver birds.

She understands he's waiting for her to speak first.

"You saw Kurt, didn't you?" she finally says. Then she stops and breathes deeply, trying to control the angry note in her voice. "He told you about the diaries."

"Yes, but you shouldn't blame him for that. He read in your message the intention to break with the code of silence behind which your aunts hid all their lives, for generations on end. Once in the know, André decided to come up here. 'She needs help,' he kept saying. Nothing could have stopped him."

As Cyril speaks, Zoe nervously stirs the fire with a stick. There's a lull in the conversation, in which he follows her movements, perhaps trying to decipher what she's silently telling him. Then he goes on. "André felt it was necessary to send you a strong signal, to inform you that we, in our way, would do the same: We'd come out, break the silence. I'd stand by him."

Zoe keeps poking into the fire, taking her time. When she speaks, her sombre tone ill-conceals a dull rage: "Is this what I'm supposed to do? Let's put Kuyper aside for a while. He's mostly interested in pushing the southern African hypothesis out there, in the big world. He has an agenda and wants to pursue it, no matter what. Let's talk about Kurt, instead. Why couldn't he keep for himself what I shared with him? Why betray me?"

"Betrayal is how you want to see it. He knew about us, about me and André, I mean. I guess he felt obliged to let us know about your plight."

"Oh, he knew about you two? So, in Gansbaai I was the only one kept in the dark!" She grimaces as she shakes her head, her eyes on her boots.

"Don't take it personally, Zoe. Look at it from another angle. In doing what he did, Kurt tried to help you. He does care a lot about you, if you get what I mean."

She keeps staring at her hands, holding the cup.

"His atonement has lasted long enough," Cyril says after a while.

She stiffens.

"What do you mean? Atonement for what?"

Cyril raises his eyes to meet the first sear of red in the sky, then frowns.

"There are things about his past very few people know. It's up to him to tell you about it."

She falls quiet.

After a long while, she stretches her hand out to him. Cyril takes it gently, as if it were a dove's broken wing. *How fragile it looks within his large palm.*

❁❁❁

The bush and the camp wake up and the spell is broken.

André comes out of his tent, mumbles a good morning, walks to the fire and grabs the kettle of coffee.

"*Dankie*," Zoe says, looking at her brother affectionately as he refills her cup. Then, with a soft smile she addresses the two men. "Stay a couple of days, even more if you wish. I'll take you around. But don't you worry: I'll manage the decamping with my team. Then, I'll be home."

André breaks into a wide smile, draws his sister to him and starts rubbing her scalp, ruffling her hair, now grown wild and untameable. "Here is my *ousus*!"

— 30 —

BENDING IN THE WIND

THE DAY BEFORE her departure, Zoe goes to the *kraal* to take her leave. She spends several hours with the elders and then with the children and the women, who present her with a farewell necklace. It has been made by interlacing an intricate pattern of ostrich-eggshell beads and dyed seeds. It's a rudimentary piece of craftwork, yet invaluable. She knows how much collective work has gone into shaping and drilling the hard shells of ostrich eggs into those tiny beads.

There's a lot of dancing and singing and laughter and tears before they let her go, before she feels ready to leave.

When she finally walks back to the camp, the bloodshot dye of the sunset is already seeping over the bush. She stares at the plain, which now, after the rains, quivers golden green at the edge of the camp. The lushness of the scene can't dispel the melancholy of the moment.

Soon I'll be gone. Most probably, never to return.

Old Koma is crouched under a camel-thorn, waiting for her. She kneels at his feet.

"You decided to stay, *Oom*."

"*Ja*. We'll die here, with our people. With our stories."

"Your stories won't die, Koma. You've been teaching the young."

"*Nee.* This time is different. When the last of our old people die, there'll be no one left who knows what life was in the time without time. Then, the slightest breeze will erase our footprints for good."

Zoe follows the old shaman's gaze and lets her eyes sway with the tall grass, savouring the perfect intimacy of their silence.

"This time I feel it's even harder to go back to where I come from, *Oom.*"

There's another long silence before Koma speaks again.

"Your steps will take you beyond worry. The shadow has been tamed now."

She looks at him, bewildered. Sensing her confusion, the old shaman adds: "It fears you now. You can keep it at bay if you want."

If I want, she murmurs to herself.

"At times, we need to be like the weed that bends in the wind," she recites. "Now I understand what you meant that day in the Karoo, *Oom.*"

The old Bushman smiles at her before drowning his ancient eyes in the setting sun.

— 31 —

THE ANCESTOR FROM LANGEBAAN

Back to Johannesburg, Zoe sends Kurt an envelope containing a short message and an almond-shaped plaster-cast object.

> *Jo'burg, March 15, 1997*
>
> *It's a copy almost as beautiful as the original, which will soon be presented to the world. Archaeologists call it a "biface." More poetically, you can consider it a chipped stone heart. Hold it in your hand and see how it fits—how it feels. This is not all I found in my wilderness, but this is the only tangible thing I brought back with me.*

"Don't tell me you're heading down there just to check on some hominid footprints discovered by someone else," Sam said half-jokingly as he bid farewell at Tsumkwe airport a few days before. "I hope you've more rewarding plans in store."

She has indeed other plans, though she wouldn't bet on their benefits. She means to confront Kurt: not so much on what she still perceives as a betrayal, but on the murky chapter in his past Cyril hinted at.

❁❁❁

She's back to the Finistère, its rituals, its smells, its dwellers: André, whom she treated so severely; Cyril, the black prince; old Georgina, the merciful. The place is unchanged. What's missing is the meek, chastened girl seeking refuge from the evils of the world in her parents' farm. That girl is gone. No need to look for her. No regrets.

❁❁❁

On the day before her visit to Langebaan, she calls Kurt to ask him if he wants to come along.

As if by tacit accord, they only exchange necessary information on the logistics of the trip. The conversation is so awkward it almost acquires a surreal tone. She asks him to drive to Milnerton; she will meet him there with Henrik Visser, the young researcher at Stellenbosch University in charge of the site. The three of them will reach their destination with her colleague's car. It means she and Kurt will not be alone in their trip. Whatever needs to be said between them will have to wait the right moment, the right setting. This time, nothing will be left to chance.

Towards the end of their phone call, Kurt breaks a piece of news: "In two days I'll be flying to Senegal for a conference of African writers."

There's a short lull.

Waiting for me while I play the role of the stubborn ascetic out in the desert: No, I could not expect this of him. Serves me right. Zoe tries hard not to let her disappointment seep through as she says, feigning nonchalance: "I doubt you could ever pass for truly African in their eyes."

"Most probably."

❁❁❁

"I'll lead the way," Visser says, stretching his arm towards the western tip of the lagoon, which lies within the West Coast National Park. Zoe and Kurt follow him past the park's entrance, walking barefoot in single file along the coast. Skirting the sandstone cliffs, they scramble up and over huge granite boulders smoothed round by the sea. The rocky vaults crop up from the sand, like domes of an underwater city surfaced millions of years ago from the ocean bottom.

They carry on for about twenty minutes until they come to an open area shaped by high dunes flanking the bay. All around, the sea water shines like melted opal.

"There," Visser says in the same casual and affable manner with which he has entertained them all along. He points his finger towards a flat sandstone ledge, hurriedly demarcated by red and white zebra hazard tape to restrict access.

They walk up to it. Zoe squats to inspect the signs more closely.

Here it is, the Langebaan trackway: just three prints, faintly discernible, showing the broad sole and narrower heel of a human being—right foot, left foot, right foot again. That's all. Yet, to expert eyes it reveals so much. "Look at this one, in particular," her colleague says, crouching down beside her and pointing at the central one. "The big toe, the ball of the foot, the arch and the heel of the foot are well discernible. Most likely a woman. About 1.5 metres tall, judging by the length of the step and given a foot length of about 23 centimetres."

"The *Homo* turned out to be a girl," Kurt whispers in Zoe's ear as he squats by her side.

"Close your eyes and picture the scene," Visser says. "Imagine going back in time 120,000 years. It's winter, heavy rain has just soaked the dune with water. A woman—a modern human anatomically identical to us—comes out of her shelter and walks down the sloping dune towards the water. A small antelope, possibly a steenbok, flees at the sight of her. We've found its spoor over there." Their guide points his finger towards another ledge.

"The woman combs the beach, looking for mussels. Later on, the wind blows dry sand on her trail, covering it. In the course of time, the proof of her passage in this world will be buried under a 10-metre thick layer of hardened sand and seashells. Only the slow forces of erosion will bring it back to the light. For us."

"This is all that remains of *Eve*'s pretty feet, then?" Kurt asks.

"Aha! I see you've been reading the newspapers' account of the finding," Visser says. "Once again, they came up with a trite African Eve's story. This time, though, if the dating proves to be accurate, we might be pretty close."

"Meaning?"

"These could indeed be the footprints of one of our earliest female ancestors."

Zoe has kept quiet, letting the men do the talking. Now she stands up and, again without saying a word, takes in the sweeping ocean views. She watches the arabesque of tidal channels and, in the distance, the turquoise water of the lagoon trapped against the beach by golden sand. All around, she doesn't detect any other human presence.

She is jealous and it's hard to admit. She has spent months digging thousands of kilometres away, in an unforgiving desert, only to come up with a chipped piece of stone, no more than a pointed amulet; while a geologist who went picnicking with his family just a few kilometres from home stumbled onto something that might change the course of paleoanthropology.

There's more to it. She thought she was immune from the need to be noted, recognized, celebrated. Remembered by posterity. While instead, all along, she's been toiling away on the same grounds. She went into the desert to offset her woes, forget her misfortunes. True. But beneath it there lay this other purpose: the chance to leave a mark. *Her* mark. Like everyone else, she could not simply ignore the greatest of human fears: the inevitable descent into oblivion. It took a bout of envy to let this final piece of truth come up.

"Well?" Kurt asks her.

"This time it will be difficult to dismiss the southern hypothesis, which locates the original home of humankind not in the Eastern plains of Africa but further down, in its southern tip," she says.

Then, making a vague gesture with her arm towards Namibia: "Which is what I was trying to prove up there. The last Ice Age dried up much of the African savannah, leaving behind pockets of habitable land. One such area is the strip of territory stretching from the Cape of Good Hope to the Kalahari Desert."

"I couldn't agree more," Visser says with a grin as he wipes off his glasses in the hem of his T-shirt. "It's high time those braggarts in British academies stop thinking that Africa boils down to Kenya and Tanzania."

❁❁❁

They are alone now. Finally. Visser has taken his leave with an excuse, wandering off the dunes to avoid—he readily guessed—being the thorn among the roses. Kurt and Zoe sit side by side on a rocky plateau, surrounded by the polished rock domes of the lost city. The muffled roar of the surf accompanies their words and, above all, their silences.

"The past always resurfaces," Kurt says as he scans the horizon. He's leaning with his back on a rock outcrop, his left arm on his bent knee. Zoe squints her eyes into the bright sunlight, breathing in the salty air. When she opens them again, it's to face him with a direct question: "Which past are you talking about: humankind's past, that of my family, or *your* past?"

She cannot conceal a note of distress—even resentment—in her voice. She's on the verge of a breakdown, right in front of *this* man, whom she doesn't really know, in whom she blindly—most probably imprudently—confided. And then there's Dario, his sweet memory, the harrowing feeling of having betrayed him for just being out here, with a stranger: so soon, so quickly.

There is a long and suspended silence, in which they both look out at sea, each seeking different things. Looking for the courage to speak out, accepting what might come with one's words.

It's such a glorious sun-day though, so unsuited to the tension Zoe feels mounting between them. She's wearing jeans and a printed silk blue blouse—one of her mother's—whose plunging neckline reveals glimpses of her cleavage. Even this seems so inappropriate now.

"I hear your frustration, Zoe," Kurt finally says, tapping his pack of cigarettes on the rock. "I owe you an explanation."

She turns her head to look at him and he locks his eyes into hers—his usual mocking sneer is gone. She craves his confession—the mutual breaking of the silence between them—but now that his words are about to come, she's afraid to receive them.

"I have never forgiven myself for what happened fifteen years ago."

The high-pitched screeching of seagulls pierces the air, almost anticipating the rawness of what he is about to reveal.

"When I started teaching at the university in London, I met Jasmine, a Vietnamese student four years younger than me. She had escaped the war in her country and lost most of her family."

Zoe looks at him, but he keeps his eyes fixed on the rock under his bare feet, as if he needs a solid point onto which to hang his words. She goes back to the image of that beautiful young woman with almond-shaped eyes and silky hair, trapped in a picture in Kurt's study.

"We got married after we had been dating for less than a year but, given the circumstances in South Africa at that time, we kept it a secret."

Kurt glances at her, then resumes his story.

"Three years after our wedding I decided to briefly return to South Africa under a false name and in disguise, hoping to make contact with the anti-apartheid underground movement," he says, his sombre voice almost drowning in the surf's sound. "They arrested me the moment I tried to get in touch with my contact. Someone, probably within my inner circle of comrades, gave me away."

Kurt pauses and mechanically pulls a cigarette out of his pack. Instead of lighting it, he puts it back.

"When Jasmine found out, she decided to fly to South Africa. I tried to dissuade her as much as I could in the brief phone calls I was allowed to make, but she was adamant. I knew nothing would stop her. She could be impossibly stubborn, but also incredibly naïve. She wanted to report my case to Amnesty International. She didn't have a clue of how the security apparatus worked."

Zoe bends her knees, pulling the legs up against the chest and wrapping her arms around them. She rests her chin on the knees, trying to make herself even smaller—no more than a blue silk cocoon abandoned on an ocean's shore, under a violent southern light.

Kurt takes a deep breath and goes on with an even more sombre, more distant tone. "At the time I was still locked up in Pretoria. My wife took a room in a hotel near the prison, hoping they'd let her see me. That same night, two men entered her room and beat her to a pulp. She died a few hours later at the hospital. They both died, she and the baby. She was three months' pregnant. I found out about her pregnancy only much later, from a letter addressed to me that she had left with a friend of ours in London."

Zoe would stop breathing if she could. Kurt's face has morphed into a mask. But the pain in his voice is all too revealing.

"The killers were never identified, but they were clearly at the behest of Hendrik van Den Bergh's office."

Another of Wilhelm's heroes.

"Security matters were censored, as you may remember. But the media often carried success stories on how the Bureau of State Security was busy protecting Afrikanerdom from the *swart gevaar* and international communism," says Kurt in a crescendo of sarcasm. After a short pause ha adds: "Well, they did not report on this one."

Kurt gazes back at the rock, his jaw tensing under the weight of those memories: "I have never forgiven myself for this. My selfishness and my unforgivable artlessness killed my wife and my child. I abandoned them to play the hero and fight to change things in this country. But change has its own dynamics: Petty, short-sighted men are of no use to it."

There is only the sound of the sea between them now, with its staccato rhythm. And yet, there is so much more. There is a wife ruthlessly murdered, an unborn child, seven years of brutal imprisonment. And, above all, an insurmountable guilt: the real curse keeping them apart.

The invisible walls Kurt erected around himself are those of a mausoleum for lasting memories. Trying to breach it would mean to desecrate a temple of perfect love. She cannot tell him what she feels. How she craves for another chance. How she is attracted to him. How she will not suppress this mounting feeling of being so fully, irreproachably alive.

Instead, she must accept she is no more than an intruder in his life—the imperfect replacement of a by-now-idealized lover. Even if he let her in, she would find herself playing the same role over and over again. For him, the past still matters more than the present. If she vanished in this precise moment, it wouldn't make any difference.

❁❁❁

The sky has suddenly dimmed, rolling in banks of dull-grey clouds. The breeze picks up, pushing back her hair. Zoe shivers in her light blouse.

"Here," Kurt says, taking off his jacket and wrapping it around her shoulders. There's a moment of hesitation on his part. They're so close ... He gently puts a hand behind her neck, caressing it ever so lightly, his eyes closed. As if he wished to make amends for the bleakness of his confession.

The first drops of rain begin to fall.

"We should go," he says, shaking out of his daze.

They follow the return path between the sandstone domes and then along the beach. The drizzle turns into a light rain. She keeps her eyes fixed on the footprints left by Kurt, who's walking in front of her.

Kurt, water dripping from his hair onto his cheeks and his white shirt, turns and helps her step over a final rocky outcrop before reaching the park exit. She grabs his hand but drops it as soon as he helps her to hoist herself. Suddenly, Zoe misses Dario—his warm, inviting smile, the radiant levity with which he faced life. But Dario is dead. And Kurt, she feels, is dead too.

Dead inside.

— 32 —

ZANZIBAR

"STRANGELY, WE KNOW less about our species than about any other hominid species," Dario wrote in his notebook. "The most important event in human evolution—the emergence of *Homo sapiens*—remains wrapped in mystery." Zoe has decided to use this quote, a tribute to her deceased colleague, to introduce the topic of her lecture at the upcoming conference. It's the least she can do to pay homage to Dario's legacy, hoping she doesn't break down when she utters his name in front of her audience. *Thank goodness we'll be in Zanzibar, away from home.*

At a symbolic level, the island represents the ideal setting to expound her thesis. Once a cradle of slavery, it will now offer a suitable stage from which to plead for the liberation of research from its last ideological and geographical shackles. Zoe will point out that archaeological efforts have been disproportionately focused on East Africa, sidelining relevant evidence coming from the southern tip of the continent. She'll corroborate the theory that the first modern people evolved in southern Africa and not in the east of the continent, as mainstream academics still maintain.

She hoped to come up with her own hard proofs. Instead, she'll have to openly admit the Kalahari denied her the striking, unequivocal discovery—a skull, if not a whole skeleton—thus teaching her a lesson against scientific hubris and vain ambition. Nonetheless, the findings at Langebaan lend enough support to the thesis of the 'alternative cradle.' What she fears most is having to descend into the academic arena to contend for it. She has always avoided the pomp and clash of big egos on the loose. She's not cut out for heated disputes, although these are part and parcel of how science progresses.

Unlike her colleagues, lodged in an anonymous chain-style hotel, Zoe has chosen an inn at the edge of Stone Town, the old part of Zanzibar City. Practically nothing has changed since her first visit ten years before. She finds again the geometric antique tiles; the hand-carved four-poster beds; the mosquito nets suspended over garden chairs for the afternoon siesta; the half-timbered balconies and the hand-crafted verandas overlooking the ocean.

Above all, she rediscovers that unmistakable Zanzibar smell: a mixture of salt water, seaweed, sun-dried fish, cinnamon, mango, nutmeg and cloves. It's the smell of life, and of restrained sensuality. Zanzibar feels like a woman who gives herself sparingly, in the secrecy of forbidden alcoves. The contrast between the moist spells of the "Spice Island" and the dry heat of the bush from which she has just emerged couldn't be starker.

Zoe looks back and marvels at what she experienced in the Namibian desert. She runs her fingers over the scratches left by the camel-thorns and relives the bush, its disarming hostility, its luring emptiness. She hears again the women singing in the night, the rhythmic step of the medicine men, Koma's stories, the laughter with which the elders dispel any tension and the quiet dignity with which they accept their destiny. They're still there, in a world so distant in time and space as to seem almost unreal. The Kalahari has left its mark, in its own right, and its memory now sings inside her—beautiful and hauntingly sad, like a Portuguese *fado.*

But even now that she's in Zanzibar, so far away from that land of thirst, there's no time to be lulled by the Tropics. Not yet. She still has to focus on her speech, which, as Kuyper hopes, will reignite the long-due debate about the true birthplace of modern humankind.

❁❁❁

"Professor Du Plessis, why are you so keen on arguing that the African Eve comes from South Africa rather than from Kenya?" asks the reporter from Dar es Salaam's *Daily News* during the press conference held after Zoe's talk. "Is this a way to emphasize the change of heart that white Afrikaners are willing to undergo in post-apartheid South Africa?"

That's the kind of question she's been waiting for. She spent whole nights under the stars of the Kalahari, thinking of how she'd answer, what she'd be willing to reveal about herself once this issue would be out in the open. All this is part and parcel of what it entails to go back into the world, among the men and women of her time. It means exposing herself, putting at stake her reputation and, being an Afrikaner, letting herself be torn apart by the ferocious adversity of moral verdicts.

"Ideally, science should be free from politics and its influence; in fact, it isn't," she says, betraying a painful weariness in her voice. "No one and no thing is immune to its tight grip. Not even some primitive bones, which over time have become its unaware victims."

Despite the air conditioning, the room feels suddenly torrid, as if she were back to her scorching desert—her mouth parched with thirst, her mind bleached by the sun. She bows her head, trying to focus and summon her strength. She can't see the people in front of her, but she senses the mounting tension coming from the floor. She gathers what forces she can to deal one more blow to a stunned audience: "Our country has finally climbed out of the darkest period of its history. Apartheid has been abolished and a democratically elected black government has been established. Now, it's time for our fossils, for years tainted by the stain of segregation, to find their way into the spotlight."

As though a weight had been unloaded from her shoulders, she raises her head and looks towards the audience. Sitting in the front row, Professor Kuyper shows unequivocal signs of discomfort. She glances over the sea of faces, gauging the impact of her words. Her eyes come to rest on a tall figure at the back of the room. Kurt holds his head high and his hands by his sides, in a relaxed but at the same time in-control posture, like a bodyguard on duty. He gives her a nod.

In the silence, only her heart is beating a crazy tune, louder and louder. Ta-tam, ta-tam, ta-tam. She shudders, fearing everyone might hear her frantic tam tam.

She takes a swig of water, a deep breath; then, articulating each word slowly and deliberately, throws her bait. "There are fossil stories from our tormented past that are not particularly flattering for the international scientific community at large."

"Could you please elaborate on that?" the same reporter asks.

Before answering, Zoe glances at Kurt, making sure he's still there. Still with her.

"In the last decades, many Western scholars have preferred to focus their research interests on a part of Africa they deemed to be politically correct—I specifically refer to the eastern regions of the continent, Kenya and Tanzania primarily. Actively encouraged by the governments of those countries, much of Western academia emphasized the importance of those areas, which are undoubtedly critical to our research, but neglected the potential, in terms of paleoanthropological relevance, that the region south of the Zambezi had already shown. What I mean is that any significant study or discovery coming from South Africa quickly disappeared into some obscure storage room. In many quarters, to publish and cite articles written by South African researchers and, in general, to study our fossils was heavily frown upon, to say the least."

Zoe has turned into a raging torrent of words, seemingly unstoppable. Even she finds it hard to recognize herself in this woman who speaks so glibly and with such unusual vehemence. "In the past, in his role as Director of our Department, on many occasions Professor Phillip Tobias officially opposed enforced segregation at universities and the restriction of academic freedom. In 1984 he flew to New York to present the Taung Child, the skull of a young *Australopithecus africanus* discovered in South Africa in 1924. The conference was organized by the Museum of Natural Sciences."

Zoe stops to take another sip of water. She clears her

voice and goes on, her eyes locked into those of the reporter. "On the day of the conference, outside the museum protesters denounced the presence on American soil of 'apartheid's fossils.' Even those unsuspecting Palaeolithic bones had been transformed into political pariahs. But we all know that the only effective boycott that brought the apartheid regime to its knees after the fall of the Berlin Wall was the economic one. I don't think that having kept South African scientists away from international academic circles greatly contributed to the fight against apartheid. I might be wrong, but isolating scholars from the global arena as a means of fighting tyranny, fundamentalism or autocratic regimes may even prove counterproductive. Be that as it may, it's high time to remove African politics from African fossils."

The reaction to Zoe's words is instant and inevitable. Each and every one seems to have something to defend or someone to accuse. Some of her fellow scientists start justifying their actions; others attack her for fostering an extremely local and limited vision of paleoanthropological research. Then there are those who call her to account about her past as a privileged white academic during the apartheid era.

"Dr. Du Plessis, what action did you take at the time to support the anti-segregationist movement in your country, at least within your academic environment?" the correspondent of *El País* asks her point-blank.

Here it is, finally, the question she has been hoping to hear and waiting to answer! Why did they take so long to come up with it? Isn't this what's expected of her, the public admission of a coward's guilt? She can still sing to herself the opening lines of that Lutheran hymn she heard on the radio so many years ago: *Let coward guilt, with pallid fear/ To shelt'ring caverns fly/And justly dread the vengeful fate/ Which thunders through the sky.*

Zoe fixes her eyes on those of Kurt before answering. She's not seeking the approval of a former political activist nor of a writer driven by his fiction. If anything, she's looking for the support of a companion, now that she's taking her first steps out of the cage of their Afrikaner heritage.

"To my greatest regret, and unlike other colleagues and friends, I did nothing. I buried my head in the sand and kept away from the real world, living in a secluded sphere of pure research. Others, many others, braver than me, acted, often incurring enormous sacrifices, to establish a sense of justice, equality and dignity in my country."

She pronounces these words in a firm, resolute tone. Then she looks down at her hands, still holding her notes, before concluding in a subdued tone: "For a long time now, I have been feeling ashamed of myself."

It's all. Her closing sentence, which Zoe scribbled on the last sheet of her notebook before taking the floor, remains only a note on paper: "We all become either victims or perpetrators—at times individually, most of the time collectively. Sometimes, depending on the circumstances and stages of our lives, we may become both."

❁❁❁

"What happened to you, Zoe? What need was there to stir up all this fuss, all this talking about apartheid, the Afrikaner, the Boer's guilt ..." Kuyper whispers vehemently in her ear as soon as the moderator closes the press conference.

Looking over Kuyper's shoulder, Zoe glances at her colleague Piet, still sitting stiffly, and meets his embarrassed stare.

"Didn't you want me to leave everyone speechless?" she says.

Outside the conference room, Kurt is waiting for her, straight and motionless like some totem pole indifferent to the elements. Zoe walks to him and touches his arm.

"You're here."

"How could I ever let you face alone these man-eating specimens of our species?" he says in his usual wry tone.

Will it always be like this, she wonders, as a wave of gratitude lifts her towards the safety buoy of his half-smile. Will he always be able to decode her moods—or needs—as if he had created them, jotting them down with his sharp-tipped pencil?

"Can you leave now or do you need to mend the mess you've left behind?" he asks, adjusting his gold-rimmed eyeglasses as he glances at Kuyper.

"I'm free, now."

"Then let's go. There's a place I'd like you to see."

— 33 —

A BALCONY OVER THE WORLD

It's late in the afternoon and the sunset light has begun to pour in, softening the view, providing a respite from the harshness of the world. They walk through a maze of narrow alleys as the muezzin's call to prayer spreads over the old town. Sitting on cement benches, men with searching eyes are playing one more game of *bao*, gossiping, chewing *qat*, lolling in the dying light. Swarms of children dart barefoot in and out of dusty courtyards. Dust is everywhere, but how different this island's dust seems to the one that sat silently over the Kalahari. Here, it swirls in joyous spiralling patterns amidst raucous manifestations of life. It infiltrates under brass-studded mahogany doors and behind thick coral stone walls. It enters all those places where people reunite to celebrate births and marriages, form alliances, break vows, stir up jealousies, debate ideas, generate new meanings. Here, dust witnesses the complex flow of human interactions.

Kurt walks briskly, touching Zoe's elbow lightly or putting a hand on the small of her back to guide her when they have to turn or take a new direction. He seems eager to reach their destination.

"Here we are," he finally says as he stops in front of a whitewashed square tower. Its façade is studded with intricately carved rosewood balconies, like henna decorations on a pale face. With his extended arm, he pushes the front door open and lets her in. They go up several flights of stairs until they reach the roof terrace, which accommodates an Ottoman-style coffee house.

Zoe suddenly finds herself in the midst of an Arabian night. Patrons are already lying on Persian carpets, resting their elbows on embroidered pillows. Rose-scented smoke rises from incense sticks while wrought-iron lanterns project glowing arabesques on gauze curtains separating a series of alcoves—islands of intimacy under the open sky.

"Zoe, meet my friend Yusuf, the owner of this place, a refined poet and wonderful storyteller," Kurt says after having hugged a stout man in his fifties with a thick black moustache. "We've spent many a night on this terrace celebrating the healing power of words."

"*Salaam aleikum.*" Yusuf greets her with a half bow, which reveals the delicate embroidery of his *kafia*. "Words are useless without a shared meal and the right audience," he says as he leads them into a corner booth. "It's always an honour to have Kurt and his friends at my table. Be my guest."

"Leave it to me," Kurt whispers. Zoe nods, grateful for this gesture of soft male authority, as the host leaves discreetly after taking their order. Once again, Kurt has sensed her mood. Right now, she wishes nothing more than to be guided, to abdicate—for once—the precepts of her reasoning mind.

A waitress, wrapped in a colourful *kanga* cloth, brings

their drinks to a low-lying rosewood table. Still standing, Kurt gestures Zoe to follow him. They lean against the stone balustrade and gaze at the sight below them. In the dimming light Zoe makes out the old town rooftops, the cast-iron columns of the House of Wonders, the palms quivering in the evening breeze, the *dhows* lulled to sleep in the harbour and, beyond it all, the ocean—opening around them like a dark embrace. Zan-zi-bar. Its name sounds like a lullaby, an evocation, an enchantment. Merely pronouncing it conjures up images of an island that, instead of being self-absorbed, locked in anxious self-sufficiency, has worked as a crossing point—or a starting point towards somewhere else. For better or for worse, in pleasure or misery, Zanzibar's paved streets have welcomed pilgrims and slave merchants, adventurers and thieves, dreamers and fugitives. Built to be outward-looking, the windows of its most sumptuous residences have been kept open towards the sea, like curious eyes waiting for what winds and fate might bring in.

Kurt slowly passes his fingers over the rough-edged beads of her wrist bracelet and Zoe emerges from her fleeting musings.

"Ostrich egg-shells. Such a rudimental material for such a fine and well-crafted object."

"The bushwomen living near the camp gave it to me, together with a similar necklace. They said it would help me to walk 'with the wind'."

Kurt continues to examine the bracelet, as if searching for signs of her life among the San.

"One day you'll take me up there," he says.

His thumb traces her lower lip, as it did that night outside his house. This time, she lets his hand continue its course along her neck and down to her breast. They kiss, picking up the ocean's breathing. Then Kurt gently pulls away from her and speaks, revealing a new tenderness in his voice.

"I wrote like a madman, for three months, day and night, revisiting what I'd been working on for the past two years and mixing it with what I found in your aunts' diaries. I wrote your story. My story. *Our* story." He pauses, trying to read the expression on her face.

She keeps quiet. Inside, she feels like deep water in a still lake. Dario's tanned face flashes for a second on its surface smiling sweetly and sadly at her, as if in a last adieu.

"For fifteen years I tried to die slowly, one day at a time," he says, his eyes now scouring the night. "But I didn't die. I'm not dead yet."

"Then, let the living take care of the living," she barely manages to say.

❁❁❁

The waitress has left on the table crispy samosas, pilaf rice and crab meat in a curry sauce before drawing the gauze curtain behind her. The food looks inviting and Zoe suddenly feels hungry. Sitting on the carpet by her side, Kurt reaches for one of the plates and offers her a well-chosen bite. She marvels at the casual intimacy of this little gesture. There is a whole atlas of emotions yet to be discovered between them.

They eat and talk into the night.

"Stay as long as you want," Yusuf tells Kurt after the last customers have left. "My attendant lives in the premises. He will let you out."

Before turning in for the night, he brings to their table a pot of boiling water for their teas.

"You never believed in the curse, did you?" Zoe asks Kurt, hugging herself, arms crossed over her chest.

"I never did," he replies a bit too dryly. "As Conrad said, this world holds enough mystery and terror and wonder in itself. The rest is mere superstition."

For the first time, she detects a weary note in his voice. *How funny*, she thinks, half-smiling, *we've just become lovers and I've already found a way to annoy him.*

"Are you cold?" Kurt asks a moment later, noticing her sudden shiver. He grabs his linen jacket lying on the pillows and puts it on her shoulders, as if with this gesture he wanted to apologize for his rather brusque reply, and at the same time brush away their past, everything that doesn't include them being together.

With the night breeze, the gauze curtains sail lightly around them, ready to take flight towards new lands.

"How does it end, Kurt?" she finally asks.

He looks at her, his mouth set in a slightly amused smile.

"I have no way of knowing. I guess we should give it a try."

She withdraws her hand, suddenly puzzled, almost lost.

"I don't mean *this*," she says, sweeping her arms out in a gesture that includes all that's there: the old town, the terrace, their alcove and their faces, barely illuminated by the only lantern still burning. "I mean the story in your book."

"Is there any difference?"

Zoe sinks her eyes into his and when she resurfaces her face shows a new glow.

"I don't know. But it no longer matters, right?"

— 34 —

ON THE PIER

IT'S NEARLY DAWN when their footsteps faintly echo through the winding streets, with the old city still fast asleep. They go past Zoe's inn and, as if by tacit agreement, reach the beach where a pier, its old timber boards bleached grey by sun and salt, juts out into the sea.

The first shafts of sunlight rise from the flat, dark land mass behind them and burst over the tall palm trees of the Shangani Gardens. At sea, the *dhows* loom white in the distance like big weary seagulls.

"It's already daybreak," he says.

"You're a writer, you can control time at your leisure, shrink it to a moment or extend it to eternity."

"Only when I write."

"Then you should never stop writing."

"That's it," he whispers as he kisses her holding her supple body.

She pulls slowly away from him and begins to undress.

Kurt watches in silence this red-haired Nereid stripping before him and in his gaze — or is it her imagination? — she catches a sudden rush of uncertainty, perhaps even apprehension.

She dives in and then turns to smile at him, her hair

dripping. Catching the early sun, her eyes flicker with green sparks, as if they no longer belonged to her but to the sea.

He quickly undresses and joins her in the water. They kiss again. Then she starts swimming. He lingers behind, watching the steady pace of her freestyle, thinking back to the times in his cell when he imagined himself gliding afar in a boundless sea.

Yes, he could freeze this moment and make it last forever. Instead, he follows her, paddling at a faster pace until he catches up with her. Then they carry on swimming side by side, looking at each other through the glistening water, losing track of each other in their thoughts, finding each other again.

Zoe spots her own shadow on the sandy bottom. It's no longer a solitary silhouette: Another one is now moving in sync with hers. Despite her growing fatigue, she feels strong, endowed with almost inexhaustible energy, as if life poured into her with every stroke. Looking back at what happened, she can now see everything crystal-clear, rushing through her mind like well-conceived sequences in a fast-forwarded movie, or in an elongated déjà-vu. She won't censor it, nor edit it. She will keep everything: the roughness, the awkwardness, the multiple shortcomings. Because this is her story. She feels water envelop her in a shiny, limitless cocoon. And, for the first time, she feels proud, worthy enough for this world.

Below Kurt, against the immense ocean floor, scenes from his life scroll by: the ball games on the lawn with his mother, the beatings from his father, the poetry by candlelight, the students killed in Soweto, Jasmine's lips, the pools of blood in the prison corridors, his unborn child, the smoky bistros in Paris. He sees himself open his black leather notebook and, in the blink of an eye, enter the sacred writing space, his pencil moving forward steady and resolute like his lover's crawl. Yes, Zoe, we shall swim like this forever, since this is how we shall live: dissolving ourselves with each stroke, and then reinventing ourselves on each yet unwritten page.

❁❁❁

From the shore, a fisherman has been tracking the two of them, two small dots suspended between the cobalt blue of the sky and the silvery slab of the sea.

On the jetty, there lies a floral print shirt held down by a black leather notebook. A light breeze blows the cover open. With invisible fingers it nervously leafs through the pages, as if looking for a specific passage, a memorable sentence. It only finds a flutter of blank paper.

Acknowledgements

NOVELS ARE RARELY written in isolation. As a writer, I feel privileged to have been able to tap into a seemingly inexhaustible supply of encouragement, linguistic proficiency and intellectual curiosity. I have to thank all the dear friends, colleagues and newly-found acquaintances who contributed to enrich and polish my writing. Among them: Jane Ball (for her editing), Archie Crail (for his writer's eye), Sébastien Doubinski (for his timely suggestions), Kathryn Pentecost (the woman in arts Down Under) and—of course—the ladies of the YVR Bookworms Club. In particular, I would like to thank Sabina Nawaz, who made me reflect about the difference between intellectual modesty and humility, and Kelleen Wiseman for her stream of consciousness.

Deserving a special mention are:
—Inez Baranay, always there when I needed a writer and mentor's shoulder.
—J.M. Coetzee, who kindly checked the expressions in Afrikaans.
—Michael Hattaway, who took the time to read the final version of the manuscript, providing most helpful comments and suggestions.

—Cecil Hershler, whose storyteller's sensibility and South African-accented voice added an extra layer of reflection and understanding.
—Saskia Waters, who read and further edited an early version of the manuscript with the eyes and heart of a Dutch-born, South African-raised palaeontologist. Like the protagonist of this book, Dr. Waters did field work during South Africa's apartheid regime; more precisely, she spent ten years at the University of Witwatersrand, of which about six were at the Bernard Price Institute for Paleontological Research.

I warmly thank Sneja Gunew and Joseph Pivato for having introduced me to my publishers at Guernica, Michael Mirolla and Connie McParland, without whom this book would not be now in your hands.

Most of all, though, I thank my husband and life-long companion, Stefano Gulmanelli, who has shared in this book from start to finish. He read my work, discussed ideas, suggested changes, challenged me when needed. No writer should be left without this kind of unwavering and invaluable support.

A final thought and thank you goes to my parents, my sister (with her endearing family) and my aunt, for just being who they are.

Having said that, I take full responsibility for any inaccuracies, mistakes, omissions or controversial views/statements contained in the text.

About the Author

In the last thirty years Arianna Dagnino has built a diversified cultural and professional experience across many borders and four continents. She was born in Genoa, Italy, and studied in London, Moscow and Boston before starting her career in journalism and international reporting, which led her to spend several years in Southern Africa and Australia. In 2010 she re-entered the academy to undertake a Ph.D. in Comparative Literature and Sociology at the University of South Australia before moving to Vancouver as a permanent resident of Canada. She is currently teaching at the University of British Columbia and, concurrently, carrying out postdoctoral research at the University of Ottawa thanks to a SSHRC fellowship. She has published books both in Italian and English on digital technologies, global mobility and transcultural flows. Among them, *Transcultural Writers and Novels in the Age of Mobility* (Purdue UP, 2015), *Jesus Christ Cyberstar* (Ipoc, 2009), *Uoma* (Mursia, 2000), and *I nuovi nomadi* (Castelvecchi, 1996). Dagnino is a member of the Writers' Union of Canada, the Literary Translators' Association of Canada and the Society of Translators and Interpreters of British Columbia.